Switch

Brenda put her arms around Brad and held him close to her, savoring a moment of togetherness. Just then Ted tapped on Brad's shoulder. "Let's switch Austins," he suggested.

"Sure, I don't mind," Brad said.

Brenda didn't let go of him. "Are you sure?" she whispered in his ear. Ted's timing couldn't have been worse.

"Sure, go ahead. I'll be fine," Brad said.

"Chris and I just thought it was time for a change of pace," Ted said.

Brenda looked at Chris and wondered how much say her stepsister really had in the matter. "So, are you enjoying the party?"

"I am now," he said. A slow Lionel Richie song began to play, and Ted wrapped his arms tightly around Brenda.

**Books from Scholastic
in the Couples series:**

MORE THAN FRIENDS

M.E. Cooper

SCHOLASTIC INC.
New York Toronto London Auckland Sydney

ISBN 0-590-40161-0

12 11 10 9 8 7 6 5 4 3 2 1   4   6 7 8 9/8 0 1/9

Printed in the U.S.A.

MORE THAN FRIENDS

Chapter 1

Chris Austin breathed in the deep fragrance of the magnolias that surrounded the old Rosemont mansion. It was late Friday afternoon, and she and her boyfriend, Ted Mason, had driven to the park for a quick date. Chris was going to her best friend's house that evening and wanted the few hours with Ted to last as long as possible. "I've always loved this place," she said as they walked around the prerevolutionary estate's overrun garden.

"I know. I don't see why we had to let Phoebe ruin our standing Friday night date, just because she decided to have an all-girl party tonight," he said, pouting.

Chris intertwined her slender fingers with Ted's, a gesture that had become second nature after a year of dating. "Oh, Ted, you know how much I love to be with you. Don't be upset over one Friday night apart — "

"I'm not upset. I suppose you're allowed *one* night away from me." There was a trace of a grin on his lips.

Chris turned from Ted and scanned the lush springtime landscape. A few of the dahlias planted by the Rose Hill parks department had wilted in the flower beds, victims of the unusually hot weather, even by Maryland standards. Chris asked, "Did I ever tell you I used to think this was a haunted house?" She pointed to the somewhat faded two-story colonial mansion that had once belonged to one of Rose Hill's founding families.

"Some people still do," Ted remarked. Then tiptoeing behind her, he whispered "boo" into her left ear.

"Ted!" she shrieked, giggling. "You scared me!"

"I'm one of the friendly ghosts — like Casper," he said, grabbing her hand and pulling her toward him. Then with a wink he added, "There's no reason to stop now, especially since we're the only ones here." The mothers and children who frequented the park during the day were long gone and it was too early for the arrival of other Rose Hill couples who considered the park their own private haven.

Chris broke loose from Ted's hold and turned her blue eyes up to his open face. "What do you have in mind?"

"You'll find out soon enough," he said impishly.

"Tease," she said. "I bet you're not thinking of anything."

"Oh, yeah?" Rising to the challenge, Ted lifted Chris off the ground and gave her a piggyback ride across the park. For a broad-shouldered, well-muscled athlete like Ted, lifting Chris was easy.

"Put me down, Ted!" she cried.

"Scared?"

"No." Chris was more surprised than scared. Ted wasn't usually this playful. It was enough to make her wonder if there really was such a thing as spring fever.

"Had enough?" he asked.

"Yes."

Ted swung her back down onto her feet. "My hero." Chris wrapped her long, slender arms around Ted's neck and pressed her lips to his. Together they fell gently to their knees and then onto the soft grass. Chris felt a warm glow suffuse her body as Ted's lips met hers.

When they parted Ted said, "Now that's what I call a hero's welcome."

"It's the least I could do — especially since I can't spend more time with you tonight."

"That's true. It is the least you can do," he said with a laugh.

Chris was glad for Ted's laughter. She'd always had a bad habit of taking things literally. But Ted's easygoing attitude kept her from getting too serious.

3

"So tell me, Chris," Ted continued, stroking the back of her neck with his fingers. "Am I still going to be your hero when you take over next fall as student body president?"

"That's got to rank as one of the all-time dumb remarks." Chris smiled as she gave Ted a playful punch on the arm. "You know the election's not going to change anything between us. That's like me saying if you throw too many interceptions next season I'm going to dump you."

"Are you?"

She was about to give him a straight answer, then realized he was teasing her again. "That's for you to find out," she said, wrinkling her nose playfully. Then before he could answer, she covered his mouth with another kiss. "Now, what do you think?"

"I think you're the best kisser in Rose Hill."

"Hmmm. How many girls have you tested to be able to come to that decision?" she wondered.

Ted answered with a raised eyebrow and another kiss. It had been a long time since Chris had felt so secure and content, she thought as she and Ted sat watching the ducks in the mansion's pond bob for their dinner. Her mind recently had been crowded with thoughts of the coming fall, when she'd take over as Kennedy High's student body president. She considered it an honor that several weeks earlier she had won a hotly contested race, which had pitted her against one of the most popular guys in the junior class. Chris lay back on the grass, feeling the cool

4

spring breeze play across her face and listening to the quiet splashing of the ducks.

The only thing that had marred Chris's happiness was the recent junior prom. Chris was gorgeous, with thick, blond hair, an All-American smile, and a body rivaling any in the fashion magazines. She had already won a school popularity contest back in October when she became Homecoming Queen. Given that victory she'd considered herself a shoo-in for Prom Queen.

But she'd gotten a rude awakening when the crown went to her friend, Janie Barstow, a quiet girl she'd considered lightweight competition. Chris had been surprised to discover within herself feelings of jealousy toward Janie, a resentment that was taking her a long time to get over. Chris even had the feeling that people thought that she had not acted as though she felt happy for Janie that night on the podium when she was elected. She was beginning to wonder if they may not be right. Chris was trying hard to recover from her defeat, but she wondered if her attitude had given her classmates second thoughts about voting her into office.

"Earth to Chris . . . you look as if your mind's on Mars," Ted said.

"No, it's right here in Rose Hill. I was thinking about next year, wondering if I'll make a good president."

"What brought this on?"

"The prom."

Ted sighed. "I thought you'd gotten that out of your system by now."

Chris plucked a blade of grass from the ground. "I haven't really felt comfortable with Janie ever since. I know she deserved to win, but I get this weird feeling in my stomach every time I see her. It's like I'm two different people."

"You'll get over it. Give yourself some time."

"I just don't want it to ruin my friendship with Janie. And I'm afraid it really could with girls like Gloria around. I ran into her today, and she told me some of the kids were calling me a spoil sport."

Ted grimaced. Gloria was the latest thorn in Rose Hill's side; she used her sharp tongue to cut down anyone who refused to pledge their allegiance to her. "Since when does anything Gloria says mean anything? I'll bet my MG she said it just to make your skin crawl."

"But she doesn't have to face being president next year."

"Now you've lost me. What does one thing have to do with the other?"

"Being prom queen's a one-night thing. It's an honor, but it doesn't hold any responsibilities. Being student body president does. I don't want anyone to think I'm in it just for the glory. I really want to do a good job."

"They'll find that out as soon as you take office."

"But there will be lots of talking behind my back between now and then. By the time fall rolls around Gloria may have said enough to totally discredit me."

"You want to know what I think?" Ted asked.

"I think you're worrying that muddled-up head of yours for nothing. Nobody takes Gloria seriously anymore. My advice to you is just to relax and have a good time at Phoebe's slumber party."

"It's a *study* party," Chris reminded him. "We've all got term papers, and finals are coming up in a few weeks. Phoebe just thought we'd get more done if we all helped one another."

"Seven girls in the same room?" Ted laughed. "I give it five minutes before the whole thing degenerates into a gab session."

"A lot you know, Ted Mason." Chris groaned as she looked at her oversized red watch. "Phoebe'd kill me if I showed up late. I think we'd better go now."

"Time out, everyone! Who wants popcorn?"

Phoebe bounded into her living room with a huge stainless-steel bowl filled to the brim with the freshly popped kernels. She plunked the bowl down in the center of her parents' glass-topped coffee table.

"It's about time. I'm starved," Brenda Austin said.

"I don't care about the popcorn," Sasha Jenkins noted, moving toward the coffee table with the five other girls Phoebe had invited to the party. "But I've had it up to here with trigonometry problems. I need a break."

"Uh, before we stop. . . . Does anyone here know how to balance the formula for hydrogen tetrachloride?" Monica Ford asked.

"Sure, I do," Chris said.

"I'd be surprised if you didn't. They'd have to kick you out of the honor society," Janie Barstow kidded.

Chris laughed along with the others as she took the notebook Monica offered her, trying to ignore the somersaults in her stomach. She thought it was silly for her to still feel so awkward around Janie. She knew she didn't have the sole franchise on beauty at Kennedy High. Yet it was still hard for her to accept that Janie had blossomed from the somewhat plain and frumpy girl she'd been at the beginning of the year into an acknowledged beauty queen.

She finished balancing the equation and handed it back to Monica. "I hope you can read my scribbling," she said apologetically. "I wrote down each step so you could see how I did it."

Monica thanked her warmly, then added, "Even after an entire year, chemistry's still a foreign language to me. The worst part of it is, though, Peter's expecting me to explain it all to him."

"That's just like a boy, isn't it?" Phoebe noted. "Out having a blast while his poor girl friend slaves over the books."

Monica grew serious. "Peter's at home practicing for an interview he's got tomorrow at WMAL."

"Don't they play old people's music?" Brenda asked. She couldn't picture Kennedy's top student disc jockey playing Frank Sinatra records.

"He's getting desperate. All the good D.C. rock stations told him they weren't about to hire a high school guy. Poor Peter." Monica sighed. "He's going to be miserable if he can't do something in radio this summer."

"Gosh, it's hard to believe summer's only three weeks away," Phoebe said, taking her fourth handful of popcorn. "How could we have let our whole junior year go by so quickly?"

"Wouldn't it be nice if they really had time machines like in the movies and we could relive the year all over again?" Sasha asked.

"You're a hopeless dreamer," Brenda said. "Would you really want to go back and relive everything?" She grabbed the ends of her long brown hair and twirled them around her fingers. "I mean maybe I'd do a rerun of New Year's Eve and my birthday, but that's it."

Chris nodded in agreement. While the plusses had definitely outweighed the minuses in her year, there had been a few rough spots she'd just as soon forget — like the time early in the fall when she and Ted nearly broke up.

Then she noticed the look on Brenda's sharp-featured profile. Seeing her now, it was hard to imagine her stepsister had had the hardest junior year of them all. Now she was one of the friendliest girls in the class, to whom everyone went to pour out their troubles. Chris liked to kid her about needing a shoulder extender to fit all the crying heads who leaned on her. She was even dating the most popular boy in the senior class. But it hadn't always been that way. Last fall Brenda had been a rebellious, sullen transfer student who'd turned pouting into an art form.

"I'd rather concentrate on the future — on really important things," Brenda continued. "Like, did I tell you Brad got us front row seats to the Madonna concert next week?"

"Only about a dozen times," Monica said with a deep sigh. "I wish I were going."

"Speaking of the future. . . . Did you get that job at the Arena Stage, Phoebe?" Kim asked, grabbing a handful of popcorn.

Phoebe nodded excitedly. "I won't be getting paid, but Woody's mom is going to let me hang out there whenever I want."

"They going to let you sing?" Kim asked.

"No, that's something she does only for Michael," Chris teased. Phoebe seemed to be spending more and more time with her voice instructor's son, another Kennedy junior.

It was hard to tell which was redder, Phoebe's hair or her blushing face. "Michael's just a friend," Phoebe said. "Really, Chris, if I just stand in the same room with a guy, before I know it you've got me going steady with him."

"Oh, you know me, Little Miss Hopeless Romantic," Chris said. She smiled innocently.

"At least I'll be doing something constructive this summer," Phoebe continued. "I imagine you and Ted will be getting his and her matching tans at the park."

"Oh, I don't know," Chris said mysteriously.

"Go on, tell them," Brenda urged, her brown eyes dancing. "You know you want to."

"Tell us what, Austin?" Phoebe demanded.

Chris wrung her hands. "It's nothing yet. The

10

other day the student government adviser, Mr. Wingate, suggested I try for an internship in Congressman Barnes's office."

"So you're going to work in D.C.?" Sasha asked excitedly.

"No. The job's in his district office. But I haven't got it — at least not yet. I just sent in the application today. I think a lot of other kids are applying, too."

"Aw, you're in for sure," Phoebe said. "Politics is right up your alley."

"But I'm not counting on it till I get it."

"How's Ted feel about the job — or haven't you told him?" Sasha asked.

"He's really great about stuff like that. He told me to go for it."

"What'll he be doing?" Sasha asked.

Chris shrugged. "He doesn't know. I told him he ought to look for a job, too. But he said something about being allergic to summer work."

"I know how to get him moving," Brenda said. "Remind him that Brad's got a job at Montgomery County Medical this summer." Her boyfriend, Brad, was a graduating senior bound for pre-med courses at Princeton in the fall.

"She's right," Phoebe agreed. "I can't see Ted sitting back and listening to a whole summer of Brad talking about how many lives he's saved."

"He's not a doctor yet," Brenda said. She tried to keep her voice light, but inside she was annoyed by Phoebe's sarcasm. Before she and Brad had become an item, Brad and Phoebe had gone out together. "He's an orderly. But

11

it's all he's talked about since he got the confirmation last week — that, and graduation, of course," she said.

Sasha cocked her head to one side and looked hard at Brenda. "Is something wrong? Either my ears are going or you sound upset."

"Oh, no," Brenda said, recovering. "Nothing's wrong."

But Chris also turned to look at her stepsister. Sasha had confirmed what she'd been thinking, too. "Are you sure everything's okay?" Chris asked.

"Hey, what is this, the Spanish Inquisition?" Brenda tried to brush off the question, but signs of her old surliness were beginning to surface.

"Yes," Chris pressed on. "If something's bothering you about Brad, maybe I can help you."

"It's really nothing," Brenda said, directing her words to the carpet fibers.

"So there *is* something wrong."

"It's hardly what I'd call a major tragedy," Brenda said. She looked around her, as if deciding whether to continue. "I can't blame Brad for being excited about graduation and looking forward to college and everything. But I'm beginning to feel like I'm getting lost in the shuffle."

Phoebe looked at Brenda. "I don't want to butt in where I'm not wanted . . ." Phoebe began cautiously, "but Brad's the type of guy who can easily take a girl for granted. He thinks that being student body president and a major hunk is all he needs to keep a girl interested. I say stand up for yourself, Brenda. When he starts coming on too

12

strong about himself, cut him down to size. He's not doing it on purpose, I can tell you that much."

"And I've seen more than enough of you two to realize he's not the slightest bit interested in anyone else," Chris added.

"I guess I'm really not worried too much about *now*," Brenda said. "But I can't help thinking about what's going to happen when Brad goes away to Princeton."

"That's months away!" Phoebe exclaimed.

Brenda wrung her hands. "I know. I guess what I'm trying to say is, I'm wondering where our relationship is going, whether we'll still be together in the fall."

"Sounds to me like you're jumping the gun," Monica said.

"No, I understand what she means," Kim interjected. "I went through weeks of worry when I moved from Pittsburgh, wondering what was going to happen with my boyfriend there."

A hush fell over the room. Everybody was well aware Kim broke up with her boyfriend shortly after the move. Kim blushed, realizing it might not have been what Brenda wanted to hear.

Phoebe broke through the silence. "Who says you can't have a great relationship with a Princeton frosh?" she said. "It's crazy to worry about it now. Let's concentrate on more important things . . . like how I'm going to lose five pounds by graduation night."

Chris looked at Brenda, and the two girls laughed. They were acting like a couple of old ladies, she realized, fretting about things that hadn't even happened yet. Phoebe was right. It was spring, the start of a gorgeous weekend, and in a little over three weeks they'd be rid of the headache of school. When it came to the things that really mattered, Chris had no reason in the world to be concerned about anything going wrong.

Chapter 2

Ted pulled his MG to a stop in front of Chris's house. His tennis racket was stowed securely in the storage space behind the driver's seat of the convertible. Whistling to himself, he hopped out and strode up the steep concrete steps to the Austins' front door. It was a beautiful Saturday, slightly warmer than the day before, a perfect day to spend outdoors with his girl friend.

He rapped the brass knocker four times, his usual knock. Before Brenda answered the door, he had time to notice the new arrangement of marigolds Mrs. Austin had planted in the pots lining the entryway.

"Hey, Ted," Brenda said as she opened the door. "Come on in."

"Nah, I'll just wait out here, thanks. Tell Chris to come on out."

"I'd like to, but I can't. She's not here."

"She's not?" Ted was clearly confused. When he'd dropped Chris off at Phoebe's house the night before he had thought they'd decided to play tennis this afternoon. "So where is she?"

Brenda bit her lip. "She didn't tell you? Well, I guess she was in a rush and didn't have time. She got a call about an hour ago from Congressman Barnes's office. The woman who's doing the preliminary interviews is being called out of town next week, so she asked if Chris could come down today and meet her. She left about ten minutes ago. You just missed her."

"I guess she missed me, too. I've been down at the mall since eleven. I'd better be going now."

Brenda shook her head. "Why don't you come on in, anyway? I've just whipped up a batch of peanut butter delights."

Ted reconsidered. He was a sucker for homemade sweets, his favorite being Chris's coconut brownies. "I suppose I can stay for a few minutes," he said, walking into the front foyer.

He followed Brenda into the kitchen. He noticed that she was wearing short red shorts, as befitted the warm weather. Physically Brenda was just about Chris's opposite. She had dark brown hair whereas Chris's was blond; brown eyes to Chris's blue; an olive complexion instead of Chris's peaches-and-cream skin; and she wore a size three compared with Chris's size seven. She also had a confidence that made her seem older than the other girls. "What would you like to drink?" she asked. Only her head was visible from behind the open refrigerator door. "We've got milk, soda, fresh lemonade. . . ."

"Lemonade sounds good." Ted sat down at the antique oak kitchen table. On the wall was a framed graphic of an array of household spices. "Is that a new picture?" he asked.

Brenda turned around. "Yeah, my mom just bought it. I'm surprised you noticed it."

"Didn't you know they call me Old Eagle Eyes?" He smiled. "Not really. It's just that I used to spend hours staring at the picture of the farmhouse that used to be there."

"That was one of Chris's mom's things. When my mother married Chris's dad, she was really hesitant about changing a lot of the stuff in the house. She's been taking her time." Brenda put a plate of still-warm cookies on the table and walked over to the cabinet to pull out two glasses. glasses.

"I wouldn't think she'd have anything to worry about. Chris seems to have accepted her."

"She does now. But every now and then Chris gets kind of sad when she remembers her mom. A couple of months ago my mom got rid of some of the curios in the china closet." Brenda sat down at the table with two filled glasses of lemonade. "Chris was really upset, because apparently they were her mother's favorite things."

Ted felt the cookie stick where the lump in his throat was beginning to form. "Really? She never told me that."

"I'm not surprised. I felt like I was pulling teeth getting the information out of her. You know how reluctant she is to talk about really personal stuff."

Ted nodded. As well as he knew Chris, he was aware that she kept a part of herself hidden from the rest of the world. A long time ago he decided he'd be better off never pressing her. He was content to wait until she was ready to tell him what was on her mind.

Brenda put down her lemonade. "Chris rushed out of here like a tornado. She didn't have time to do anything but change her clothes, put on some makeup, and race downtown."

"I'm sure she'll call me just as soon as she gets back," he said, reaching for another cookie. "Mmmm. These are really good."

Brenda smiled in appreciation. "Thanks. It's my own secret recipe. I've been making them since I was a kid. In fact, this batch is part of the care package I'm bringing to Garfield House tomorrow. Did Chris tell you I'll be working there full-time this summer?" Garfield House was a Washington halfway house that Brenda had found shelter in when she ran away from her mother a year earlier. The counseling she got there had helped her weather that storm and the other problems in her life. Since then, she spent weekends and afternoons there, helping other people cope with their troubles.

"No," he said, washing down the cookie with a large gulp of lemonade. "So both Austin women will be working this summer."

"Why don't you look around for a job?"

Ted shook his head. "I really can't see myself in one of those McDonald's uniforms. Besides, I figure this'll be the last summer I'll ever be able to take it easy. But it's going to be lonely if Chris gets that job."

"What about sports?" Brenda asked.

"Football doesn't start till fall," he pointed out.

"But there's baseball. I've noticed some signs around town for a summer league."

"What signs?"

"They're all over town — there are open try-outs this week."

Ted shrugged. "I don't know. I haven't played in a long, long time."

"Who knows? It could be fun," she said.

"Maybe," he said, rising. "Thanks for the cookies — and the company. And ask Chris to give me a call as soon as she gets back."

As Ted drove back to his house his eyes were drawn to the yellow posters tacked on almost every telephone pole. He would never have given them a second thought if Brenda hadn't planted the bug in his ear. But there they were, announcing the upcoming tryouts for the County Summer Baseball League. Hmmm, he thought to himself, I wonder what it'd be like to play after all these years.

Chapter
3

"What are you doing here?" Chris gasped. It was Monday morning, and she'd just run out of her fifth period classroom and into Ted's rock-hard chest.

"Well, if you're not happy to see me I'll leave." He pretended to pout, but he was such a bad actor Chris couldn't help laughing. "Okay, so I won't leave," he said, wiping his forehead with the back of his hand. "It's so hot in here Kelsey let us out of class three minutes early. I thought I'd walk you to lunch."

Slowly they began to wind through the crowded noontime hallway toward the second floor stairway. It wasn't easy. It wasn't just the sticky heat of the building that made it so difficult. Every few feet someone would wave or shout hi or stop to say a few words. Ted was used to it, as the star quarterback on the football team. Chris, too, had always been popular, but she still wasn't totally used to having so many people recognize her as study body president.

"Have I told you how beautiful you look today?" Ted asked.

"Boy, am I lucky to have a guy like you. I'm a wreck, Ted," Chris answered.

"I mean it, though. I like what you did with your hair, piling it up on your head like that."

Chris almost laughed again. She'd overslept that morning and hadn't had time to fix her long, straight blond hair. Almost as an afterthought she'd twisted it up on the back of her head with a blue butterfly clip.

The crowd finally thinned as they walked down the stairs toward the cafeteria. When they reached the landing that separated the two banks of steps halfway down the stairwell, Ted reached out and grabbed Chris by the waist. Pulling her close, he began to kiss the back of her neck.

"Not here," Chris whispered, scampering away down the steps. Her voice was insistent without being reproachful. "Someone might see us."

"So what? We're not exactly having a secret affair." Quickly, he joined her at the bottom of the stairwell and sneaked in a kiss on the cheek.

This time Chris didn't complain. "You're irrepressible, Mason. It's funny how after all these months together I'm still not used to public kisses. But I'm trying."

Ted led her through the cafeteria door. "It's

hard to undo sixteen years of your father's police tactics."

"Ted!" Chris exclaimed. "Don't talk about Dad like that. He's always saying how much he likes you."

"That's only because he found out what a great football player I am," Ted smiled. "Only kidding. He's all right when you get to know him."

"But being a good athlete hasn't hurt you, Ted." Chris winked at him as she carried her tray out to her favorite bench on the quad outside the cafeteria. She smiled as she spotted Phoebe, Woody, Kim, Brad, and Brenda, who'd all beaten her there.

"Hi, gang," Chris said as she gently placed her tray on the weatherbeaten bench, next to Phoebe's.

"Chris, we've been taking an informal poll," Phoebe said. "As you're about to find out, it's about a hundred and eight degrees out here. . . . Well, maybe not that much, but it's pretty hot. And it's not much cooler inside. Don't you think they ought to close the school?"

"What's the vote so far?" she asked.

"Five to nothing," Brenda called out.

"Make that six," Ted said as he sat down next to Chris. "It ought to be unconstitutional to make us sit in there when the air conditioner's on the blink." He turned to Brad. "You're still our official leader. Isn't there something you can do?"

Brad put down his roast beef sandwich. "As

Chris is about to find out, the student body president has a lot of prestige but not much clout. All I can do is complain."

"Why don't we?" Chris asked. "We could draft some petitions, present them to the administration. Let them know what we think."

Phoebe leaned over and stared at Chris. "What are you looking at?" Ted asked.

"Just checking if that really was Chris talking."

"Hey, I'm not turning into a revolutionary on you. But we've got a right to protest. It's called the First Amendment."

"Sounds like you've been studying for your government final," Woody said.

"More like practicing for her interview for Congressman Barnes's job," Brenda added.

"It doesn't matter," Brad interjected. "The school board would say we were a bunch of kids who don't want to take finals."

"Well, aren't we?" Woody asked.

"You poor juniors think you've got it rough. What about us seniors?" Brad asked. "Why should we have to take tests when we've already been accepted by colleges?"

"Why bother coming to school at all?" Woody asked.

"What else would he do all day?" Ted asked.

"You're right," Woody said. "Knowing Davidson, he'd just start studying for his pre-med classes."

"I don't know how you can think of being a doctor, Brad," Kim said, wincing. "The sight of blood makes me sick."

"What are you trying to do, Kim, ruin my appetite?" Woody asked.

"Nothing could do that," Chris noted with a twinge of jealousy. For all the food Woody ate he never got fat. "But I've got a favor to ask you, Brad. I'm going to need a rundown on all the ins and outs of student government. When can we get together?"

"How about tonight?"

"Sounds fine," Chris said. "Your place or mine?"

"Why don't you come over around eight?"

"Uh, Brad." Brenda tugged at the sleeve of his red plaid shirt. "Don't you remember? We're going out tonight."

Brad slapped the table. "See, the heat is making my brain melt. I'm sorry, Bren," he said. "Of course, we're going out. But, Chris, how about if I drop by about fifteen minutes earlier? That ought to give us enough time to get started."

Chris looked first at Brenda, then seeing the smile return to her face, she nodded. "That's fine, Brad."

"I'd like to hear more about this job with Barnes, too. It sounds great," he added.

"Real world politics," she said. "The woman I spoke with the other day told me I'd be doing stuff like answering the phones and filing. The district office helps people figure out which government agency they're supposed to deal with for different problems. It also handles complaints about federal regulations, pollution, crime, stuff like that . . . not to mention speaking engagements for the congressman. It's a small office but pretty busy." She quickly raised her hand to her mouth. "What am I saying? I'm talking like the job's already mine."

"You were born for that job," Woody said.

"Let's not jinx it, Woody," Chris said. "I'm not going to think about it anymore — at least not till they call me back for another interview. This time I'm not taking anything for granted."

Brad turned toward Ted. "So while Chris is training to be our next congresswoman what are you going to be doing, Ted — swimming laps at the pool?"

"No." He paused. "I'll be at Briarwood Park playing baseball."

Chris nearly choked on her tuna salad. "You will?" she gulped. "When did this happen?" She was a little hurt he hadn't told her before springing the news on the gang.

"This morning, really. For the past few days, I've been noticing those posters on all the telephone poles. You know the ones — announcing tryouts for the summer community leagues. I thought to myself, there's got to be a reason I'm so drawn to them. Then I decided why not give it a shot? It ought to be fun knocking around the old ball. I haven't played on a team since junior high little league."

"I think it's great," Chris announced, smiling. Now that the surprise of the announcement wore off, she realized this was the best news she could have heard. She gave him a big hug, right in front of everyone.

"It's got to beat sitting around doing nothing," he admitted, "especially since you all seem bent on leaving me out of the action with all your fancy jobs."

"Oh, Ted, don't put it that way," Chris interjected. "Look at the favor you'll be doing yourself. Think of the jump you'll be getting on football season. Playing baseball ought to get you in good shape. You going to pitch?"

Ted shook his head. "Throwing a baseball and a football are two different things. I'm not interested in pitching. The thing I like best about baseball is hitting."

"I can see it now," Woody said, looking up into the cloudless sky. "Bases loaded. Two out. It's the bottom of the ninth. Your team is down by a run. They're counting on you, Mason. You step up to the plate. Strike one, right down the middle. You glare at the pitcher. He spits on the mound, then fires a ball waist high. Strike two. That gets you mad. So you step out of the batter's box, rub your hands together, and march back up to the plate with determination written all over your face. Then the pitcher winds up, lets go of the ball . . ." He paused dramatically.

"Then I hit it over the fence for a grand slam homer." Ted grinned.

"Nope. Called strike three. End of game. You lose."

Ted hooted good-naturedly. "It was a bad call,"

he said with conviction. "I'd like to see you swing a bat, Webster."

Woody made a show of adjusting his collar. "I once got a single playing softball in PE," he offered.

Everyone laughed. Woody's lank body was more suited to dancing than playing baseball. Chris remembered when he'd once told her he broke out in hives at the very mention of the word *sports*.

"I never knew you were that interested in baseball," Chris went on. "You don't even watch the Orioles on TV."

"I hate spectator sports," Ted replied. "But I like playing. I kind of wish I'd thought about it sooner. It would have been more fun playing varsity this spring."

"Yeah, they could have used you," Brad said. "Two wins and fifteen losses. They reeked." He pinched his nose.

"The competition was pretty rough this year," Ted said in the team's defense. "Anyway, I'll get a chance to play with a lot of the guys this summer. Justin Pratt told me he and most of the starters will be in the league, too."

"Think you're going to win the batting title?" Woody asked.

"Hey, don't rush things. All I care about is having a good time," Ted said.

As Chris finished her lunch she continued to steal looks at Ted. He looked so excited about playing baseball. Her happiness was marred only

27

by the knowledge that Ted had announced his plans to the crowd before telling her about them. But at least he wouldn't be depending on her completely to make the summer fun. With the job in the congressman's office — if she got it — and the student council to organize, she wasn't going to have a lot of time just for fooling around. And it wasn't clear that Ted realized that yet.

Chapter
4

The following afternoon Chris sat down on the top row of the old wooden bleachers at Briarwood Park, a block-long field near the downtown business district. Squinting her eyes against the glare of the bright afternoon sun, she needed only a few seconds to spot Ted among the fifty or so boys crammed onto the two baseline benches on the field just beyond the wire mesh fence across from her. It was the first day of tryouts for the league. Chris stared right at Ted, and, as if some mental communication were being transmitted, he looked up, spotted her, and waved. She waved back, glad to see he wasn't mad at her for being late.

It had been a busy afternoon. Earlier in the day Chris found out that plans for the honor society's end-of-the-year banquet were in shambles. The restaurant they'd reserved had canceled, the girl who'd been in charge of making the arrangements had quit the planning committee. As president of the honor society Chris had no choice but to take on the responsibility. So she spent the better part of an hour on the phone calling every restaurant in town, only to discover it was too late to reserve space for the banquet that was planned for the following Friday night. She had been about to cancel the banquet when the perfect solution dawned upon her: The honor society could hold the banquet at her house. She was even able to get Kim and her mother's catering company, Earthly Delights, to agree to prepare the food. Now all she had to do was ask her parents.

Chris was so wrapped up in her thoughts and wondering when Ted was going to join the boys now playing on the field that she was jolted a little when Allison Pedrosia, a girl in her Spanish class, moved up from the lower part of the bench to sit next to her.

"In case you're wondering, you haven't missed much," Allison said. "The coach made all the guys do calisthenics first."

"Hmm, I wouldn't have minded seeing all those gorgeous bods work up a little sweat," Chris said.

"Don't worry, there'll still be plenty of action," Allison said, squinting up at the bright sun. "I sure wish I'd worn my bathing suit."

"Me, too," Chris said, rolling up the sleeves of her striped shirt. "And some suntan lotion. I burn easily." She turned back to the brunette next to her. "Is Walt trying out?"

"That's him pitching," Allison said proudly. Her boyfriend, Walt Weston, was known as Mr. Shakespeare in Chris's English lit. class. "Unfortunately, so far, he hasn't been doing so hot."

Now, down on the field, Chris noticed an older man, probably the coach, saying something to the nine boys on the field. Ted was still on the bench, his head turned toward a tall, brown-haired boy who was approaching the batter's box. Ted was scowling. Chris looked at the other boy again. "Do you know who that guy is?" she asked Allison.

The girl's straight black hair formed an umbrella over her shoulders as she shook her head no. "Never saw him around Kennedy. Probably a guy from Leesburg or someone home from college." Allison grinned. "He's kind of cute — but don't tell Walt I said that."

Meanwhile the boy swung mightily at the first pitch Walt threw him. The ball sailed away over the center fielder's head and dropped into the adjacent field. A home run. The boy loped around the bases in a graceful trot, as if hitting a homer were as routine as breathing to him. Chris turned back to look at Ted, who was rubbing his left sneaker into the ground as if he could erase what had just happened.

"Poor Walt." Allison sighed aloud.

Another batter stepped up to the plate. He was among the many boys Chris recognized from Kennedy: Bobby Adler, the varsity's starting first baseman. Ted was staring at him intently, leaning forward, his elbows resting on his knees.

31

Bobby took two balls before hitting a single between the shortstop and the second baseman. The coach then replaced Walt with Kennedy's star pitcher, Justin Pratt, and called Ted up to the plate.

Confidently, Ted walked toward the batter's box. Chris held her breath as he took a few practice swings. She wasn't an expert on baseball, but she was impressed by the ease with which he swung the bat. In his strong hands it looked as light as a fly swatter.

Ted got into his hitting stance, gritting his teeth and taking on the slightly ferocious look Chris remembered from football season. He swung at the first ball and missed. Now Chris gritted her own teeth. He hadn't looked good. Several guys on the bench were hooting, the brown-haired boy louder than anyone. Chris thought that was unfair, not to mention unsportsmanlike. Ted was obviously trying his best.

He looked even more determined to hit the ball on the next pitch. But the ball was so wide of the batter's box he didn't make a stab at it. Chris thought that may have made him overanxious to hit the next pitch, which he missed for strike two. That left him only one more chance to connect with the ball. Looking almost desperate, Ted swung, and missed the next pitch, and struck out.

Chris felt so bad for him she wished she could run down on the field and throw her arms around him. He looked defeated — shoulders sagging, head bent in the same dejected stance he had whenever he passed the football for an interception.

"Ted's taking it so hard," Allison commented.

"Oh, he'll get over it," Chris said. "He always does. I see Walt's looking pretty relaxed."

Allison laughed. "Look at him. Could a klutz like Walt really take this game seriously? He just came out to have a good time."

Chris spotted Ted back on the bench, looking lost in thought. He didn't look back up at her until the coach tapped his shoulder and ordered him into the outfield. Ted reached under the bench for the glove he had brought from home and jogged away.

Chris was hoping he'd make a spectacular catch just to show those other guys they weren't dealing with a loser. But it wasn't Ted's day in the field either. The third boy in the batting order hit a ball right at him, which Ted caught — and then let fall out of his glove. Chris was too far away to see his face, but she could imagine how embarrassed he was. She knew that she felt embarrassed for him. Chris was thankful he didn't get any other chances to test his fielding.

About an hour later the coach called it a day and told everyone he would be holding tryouts for three afternoons before assigning the players to teams.

Chris ran up to Ted as soon as the coach was finished. He smiled, though he also said, "You think you can stand being seen with Mr. Slippery Fingers?"

"Come on, Ted, you didn't do so badly," Chris said in her most soothing voice. She slipped her arm through his, and they began to walk slowly to his car.

"Who are you kidding? I didn't exactly wow them out there."

"But it's only the first day."

He nodded. "I know." Then cheering up a little, he added, "I'm not really as worried as I sound. I just wish I had done better with you watching me."

"Since when do you have to impress me? I don't hang around with you because of your baseball skills."

"It's a good thing. At this rate, I'd probably never see you again."

"Ted, stop talking like that," she said, alarmed at the defeated tone of his voice.

He laughed. "Just kidding. Believe me, you're not going to see a repeat performance of today's disaster. I guess I should have expected it. I haven't played ball in years."

"By the way, who was the guy you were speaking to on the bench?"

Ted smirked. "Him? That's Terry Detroit. Name ring a bell?"

Chris looked at him blankly. "No."

"He's a defensive end on the Leesburg football squad. You'd never know to look at him, but he's a pretty mean blitzer." Ted rubbed the back of his neck, as though he were reliving the pain of the tackles. "So I introduced myself, trying to be friendly and all. But the guy's a real jerk. He had to bring up the General Lee incident — and my part in it."

Chris couldn't help wincing. At the Kennedy-Leesburg game in the fall, Ted and some other football players had painted the statue of Robert E. Lee that was the pride of the Leesburg campus.

"What'd he do?"

"He asked me where my paintbrush was and started to razz me when I got up to hit."

"Maybe you were trying too hard . . . trying to prove something to him."

Ted nodded sheepishly.

"Oh, Ted, I wish you wouldn't act that way. It doesn't prove anything."

"You're right. Besides, he got lucky today. Walt can't pitch. But I'll have all summer to set him straight."

"But won't you end up wanting to cooperate with him? I mean, you'll be teammates and all — not rivals."

"Maybe not. I found out Rose Hill's got two teams in the triple-A division, the Reds and the Yankees. Kennedy guys usually get slotted to the Yankees, and preps, college guys, and guys from other schools get put on the Reds. So we'll probably be playing against each other."

"If that's the way the teams line up how come the coach didn't assign everyone today?"

" 'Cause not everyone there will make the triple-A league. Guys like Walt will wind up in the lower divisions, where the competition isn't so tough."

35

"So you have no guarantee you'll make the Yankees?"

Ted gave her an okay sign. "The coach knows I'm a Kennedy athlete. I don't have anything to worry about."

"But don't you think you'd better take the coach's advice and practice?"

Ted cupped her chin in his palm and tilted her face so that their eyes met. "Worried about me, huh? I told you, what happened today's not going to happen again."

Chris put her hands around his. "I'm just speaking from experience. I mean, look at me. I thought I had the prom queen election all sewn up, too," she reminded him.

He kissed her lightly on the lips. "You had my vote. I can't help it if the rest of your class has no taste."

"That's sweet." Chris smiled up at him. "All I'm saying is that it's not a good idea to take stuff for granted."

Ted kissed her forehead. "You're such a worrier. But that's one reason I love you, I guess. I know you've got my best interests at heart, but believe me I'm not going to lose any sleep over this — so don't you, either. It's all going to be a piece of cake. You'll see."

Chapter 5

Chris had been debating with herself all afternoon about how to bring up the subject of the honor society banquet with her father. She finally concluded it was best to get it over with as soon as she could, so she broke the news over dinner that evening. " . . . so you see, Dad, I really had no choice. If we can't have the banquet here, we can't have it at all," she concluded. She waited expectantly for her father's reaction.

Mr. Austin, seated at the head of the rectangular dining room table, lifted his linen napkin to his mouth. He looked across the table to his wife. "Fine dinner, as usual, Catherine," he said. Then, turning sharply to his right, he said, "You should have checked with us first, don't you think, dear?"

"There wasn't time," Chris fretted. She picked up one of the crystal goblets her stepmother liked to use for everyday dining and took a big gulp of ice water. She looked over pleadingly at her stepmother.

Mrs. Austin winked at Chris. "It's all right with me," she told her husband, "as long as Chris keeps her word that she and her friends will do all the cooking and cleaning up."

"It's the principle of the thing," Mr. Austin said as he helped himself to a second helping of roast beef and mashed potatoes. "I don't like the idea of kids riding roughshod through my house — "

"Dad, I've had parties before," Chris interrupted. She couldn't believe her father would actually say no. She looked across the table at Brenda, but her stepsister just blinked at her helplessly. Chris understood Brenda's reluctance to get involved. After months of trying, she was only now beginning to feel accepted by her demanding stepfather, and she couldn't risk doing anything to snap that fragile bond.

But Chris did get reinforcement from an unexpected source: Brad, whom Brenda had invited to dinner that evening. "Excuse me, Mr. Austin," Brad interrupted. "I'm in the honor society, too, and I can assure you we're not your typical bunch of rowdies. You don't have anything to worry about."

Mr. Austin looked at Brad. "I say it's none of your business, son."

"Daddy!" Chris let her fork clatter down on the bone china.

"That's okay, Chris. Mr. Austin, I'm sorry if

I stepped out of line, but Chris was stuck with an impossible situation, and now she's come up with a perfectly feasible solution."

Mr. Austin was quiet for several seconds. Chris tried to calm her nerves by slowly counting the flowers on the wallpaper on the opposite wall. Finally her father said, "All right. Go ahead. I know I can trust you. But please don't ever do this again."

"Thanks, Dad." She got up and hugged her father. Then she sat down and smiled across the table. "Thanks, Brad." She saw Brenda smile as well and reach for Brad's hand under the table.

"Any time," he said as he reached for another dinner roll. "But I really meant it about your doing a good job today."

"I just did what I had to," Chris said.

"Don't downplay yourself. You showed just the right kind of quick thinking that's going to make you a good student body president."

"I've got two pretty big shoes to fill," she said. "You managed to accomplish an awful lot this year."

"This mutual admiration society's enough to give a girl a sugar rush," Brenda said. She made a gagging gesture with her spoon.

"Brenda!" her mother admonished her.

Brad picked up his water glass. "Here, take some water to dilute the effect," he said. "I know I got a little carried away. But I feel bad that Chris's gone to all this trouble and I won't even be able to make it to the banquet."

"Why not?" Chris asked.

39

"It's the night of the Madonna concert." He shrugged. "I'm as gung-ho about school stuff as anyone, but a guy's got to draw the line somewhere."

Brenda let out a deep breath. "I'm glad to hear that. I was beginning to have visions of exchanging our front row seats for a recital of Hamlet's soliloquy."

"Hey, the honor society's banquet is not that dull," Chris said. "It's going to be just as much fun as a regular party." Turning to her father, she added quickly, "Only not as loud."

"I can't believe school's almost over," Brad said wistfully. "Yesterday was the last government meeting. Next Monday we're having the annual senior day breakfast. I wish it could go on and on."

"Not me," Brenda said. "I can't wait for summer to start."

"Wait till next year. You'll change your mind." Brad gulped down his glass of water. "Do you realize in a little over two weeks my high school career's going to be coming to an end — a whole era of my life? When I think about all the time I've wasted. . . ."

"Like when?" Brenda wondered.

"Nothing specific," he said. "But when I was a freshman it seemed as if high school would last forever. Now that it's almost over I look back and wish I'd savored the good times more. But at least I can make the most of the days I have left — live each minute to the fullest. Know what I mean?"

"Brad, does that mean you won't have time to

spare to finish filling me in on how to win the support of the student reps?" Chris asked.

"I think I can manage to squeeze in a few minutes for that," he told her. "How about tomorrow evening?"

"Fine with me."

"Great, then — "

"Wait, Brad," Brenda cut in. "We're going to Duane's house to help plan his grad night party."

"How could I have forgot about that?"

"No problem," Chris said. "We can do it some other time. We've got all summer — though if my job comes through I'm going to be tied up a lot."

"Yeah, how about that, Mr. Austin, having your daughter work for Congressman Barnes. It's some honor, huh?"

Brenda squeezed Brad's hand gratefully. He cared so much about other people and came through for her so many times, she couldn't believe she'd once thought he occupied that place in the stratosphere reserved for the lofty, unapproachable types — like rock stars and pro tennis players. But after talking with him, she realized how silly it was to jump to conclusions like that. He was caring, sensitive, and easygoing — those qualities that had made him so popular in the first place. Brad had turned one of the worst years of Brenda's life into one of the best.

"Instead of sitting here and watching TV, let's go somewhere special," Brenda suggested as she and Brad rose to leave the dinner table.

Brad glanced at his T-shirt and khaki pants. "I'm not really dressed for a trip into D.C.," he said.

"D.C.'s not the only place I'd call special," she teased, with just a trace of a grin on her face.

"What do you have in mind?" he asked, his brown eyes opening wide.

Brenda linked her arm in his. "How about Rosemont Park? You said you wanted to make each day from now on one for the record books."

Brad looked at her curiously. "How long have you been planning this?"

"I just thought of it. Tonight is the beautiful beginning of the beautiful end of your Kennedy High career."

As they walked toward Brad's car, the sun was setting behind a bank of clouds, casting a raspberry glow in the early evening sky. Brad started up the car and turned on the radio. The D.C. station was playing a song from Sting's latest album. Brad reached down to turn the tuning knob, but Brenda grabbed his arm before he could touch it.

"Keep it on," she requested.

"He's so whiny," Brad complained.

"I like this song," she told him.

"You have strange taste."

"No, you do," she said. Then she began to giggle. It had become a running joke with them. Every time they got into Brad's car the same thing happened. One or the other would complain about the music. Brad liked mellow, light pop hits. Brenda considered herself more musically adventurous, interested in lots of different styles.

"I've got an idea. Let's compromise." Brad opened the compartment under the armrest and pulled out a Madonna cassette.

"Did you ever wonder what you'd be like if you had grown up here in Rose Hill? I mean, do you think we'd have connected?" Brad asked.

"I wouldn't have been the same person. Growing up in Washington made me different."

"But only superficially. We're the same where it counts." He rapped the spot over his heart a few times. He lifted his arm across the armrest and rested it on her thigh. "I know why you wanted me out of there," he told her. "I spent too much time talking about Chris — and not enough about you."

"That's not true," she protested, blushing slightly.

"Oh, it is," he said. "I didn't mean to leave you out — that gung-ho school spirit side of me took over, I guess. It may sound silly, but I feel a responsibility — Chris will be my replacement next year. I want to make sure she gets off on the right foot."

"Well then, your timing was perfect, Davidson."

"Hey, I didn't mean to get your stepfather all steamed up."

"I don't mean him. Chris needed the lift tonight. She was watching Ted at those baseball tryouts this afternoon. He didn't do so hot."

43

"What's the matter? Did he only hit one home run?" Brad joked.

"I mean he really didn't do well. On top of that some guys were ragging him. Chris came back as mad as if they'd insulted her."

Brad began to chuckle. "Chris always takes things too seriously. Guys knock each other all the time. It's no big deal. I'll bet anything he's not in as bad shape as Chris thinks. In fact, I think I'll go check him out myself. You ought to come, too. Ted always does well when he's got a cheering section."

"You sure he'll want us around? Chris said he was pretty rusty."

"Don't worry," Brad chided her. "I know Ted. He always pulls through when he's got his friends rooting for him."

Soon afterward they arrived at Rosemont. Brenda led Brad to her favorite spot under a large weeping willow on the pond's south side. "Let's forget about Ted and Chris," Brad whispered in her ear. "I've got something more important on my mind."

"What's that?" she asked.

"Us." He sat down on the soft carpet of grass and patted a spot next to him.

Brenda needed little convincing. The white lights atop the mansion shone through the willow branches, casting mysterious, inviting shadows on Brad's smiling face. Brenda dropped to her knees, then lay down beside him. He picked up a stray willow branch and twirled it between his thumb and forefinger. Raising his eyebrows in a devilish arch he said aloud, "Anyone here ticklish?"

Brenda's eyes opened wide. "Oh, no!"

Before she could react, Brad flicked the branch all around her waist and made her break into uncontrollable laughter. When he realized she had had enough he tossed away the branch and silenced her giggles with a long kiss.

Her brain seemed to shut itself off and she let herself just enjoy the sensation of the moment. She and Brad had created their own special world that was far removed from everyone and everything else. As she opened her eyes and looked up at the stars twinkling their greetings down at her, she thought there couldn't be a luckier girl anywhere in the universe.

Chapter
6

"Mason! Ted Mason!"

Chris looked over from her spot at the top of the bleachers to see Brad yelling to Ted on the field and leading Brenda, Phoebe, Woody, and Peter toward her. "Hi, guys. Welcome to the Ted Mason fan club." She smiled.

Phoebe sat down in the space next to Chris. "Hey, did any of you bring suntan oil? It's hot out here."

"No, but I snagged some cookies from the cafeteria," Woody said. He turned around from the bench below and waved a cellophane-wrapped package in front of her nose.

"Thanks." Phoebe started to reach for it but then pulled back her hand quickly, as if removing it from a flame. "Take them away. They'll ruin my diet." Immediately she jammed a piece of sugarless bubble gum in her mouth. It was a poor substitute, but definitely less fattening.

"Your loss is my gain," Woody said, biting into one of the cookies. "Watching baseball always makes me hungry."

"It's not a real game." Chris pointed to the field. "They're not even keeping score."

"I don't care," Phoebe said, adjusting her white sun visor over her eyes. "It's spring. The sun is shining. Tons of gorgeous boys as far as the eye can see. I'm staying."

Brenda, who was sitting on the other side of Chris, reached down and snagged a cookie from Woody. "Thanks," she said. "Say, Chris, did you hear what happened to Gloria Macmillan today? Ms. Alpert caught her smoking in the girls' locker room. She gave her detention."

"That makes two in a row," Chris said. "I can't think of anyone who deserves it more."

"Hey, I see Ted!" Woody shouted.

"Call me when he gets up to bat," Peter Lacey said. He stretched his long legs onto the bench below him, tilting his face up toward the mid-afternoon sun. "I'm going to catch some rays."

"Some friend you are, Lacey," Brad said. He tried to push Peter up into a sitting position, but Peter wouldn't budge.

"I'm here, am I not?" Peter protested.

"Yeah, Brad, you know how hard it is to pry him away from that radio station of his," Woody noted.

"What are you going to do when WKND goes

off the air for the summer, Peter? Any leads on the D.C. stations?" Brad asked, plopping down next to him.

Peter was still facing the sun. "I haven't given up yet. But I'll tell you this. You won't find me groveling to Laurie Bennington to get her dad to give me a job at his TV station. I'll work at Burger King before I get that desperate."

Chris's attention was drawn from the boys' conversation by a movement down on the field. Ted had jumped off the bench and was yelling at the Leesburg boy. Phoebe tugged at the sleeve of Chris's rugby shirt. "What's going on down there? Who's that guy, anyway?"

"Someone from Leesburg. A guy named Terry. He was giving Ted a hard time all afternoon yesterday."

"Looks like he's planning to keep it up today," Phoebe observed wryly. "Too bad. He's kind of cute."

Chris sighed. "I don't know why Ted can't try to get along with that guy. Just because he's from Leesburg doesn't mean they've got to be enemies for the rest of their lives."

Brad overheard her. "That's Terry Detroit, isn't it? If I were Ted I'd hate him, too. He practically bashed Ted's head in last fall."

"Men!" Chris shook her head.

"Okay, everyone. Quiet." Brenda announced. "Ted's coming up to bat."

The bleachers were silent as Ted took his practice swings. Chris was so nervous she had to remind herself to keep breathing. *Please don't*

48

strike out, she whispered to herself, hoping Ted could read her silent message. She noticed that he looked up at the stands as he walked to the plate, but this time he didn't acknowledge her presence.

With his jaw clenched and his eyes glued on the pitcher, Ted got into his batting stance. This time he was more patient, letting two balls go by before taking his first swing. Ted fouled the next pitch behind the backstop. Chris let out a deep breath, grateful he had at least been able to make contact with the ball.

Brad stood up and shouted, "C'mon, Ted. Sock it out of here. You can do it, buddy!"

"Be quiet!" Chris hissed.

Brad turned around. "Why? I'm letting him know we're behind him."

Chris was still looking at Brad when Ted took his next swing. But she heard the sound of the ball smack against the bat, and she jumped up in time to see it sail into the outfield. It was a line-drive single.

"Way to go, Mason!" Brad raised his fist in the air triumphantly and turned back to Chris with a smug look on his face.

Chris was sorry that she'd shown so little faith in Ted. I should be his number one cheer-leader, she told herself. Then she jumped up and shouted, "Go get 'em, Ted!"

Ted looked up at the group and blew Chris a kiss. The next boy hit a single into right field. Ted zoomed past second base and slid easily into third. He got up, brushed the dust off his jeans, and flashed a thumbs-up sign to his friends. Chris was delighted. Ted was going to do fine, after all.

"I think he's going to try to steal home," Brad said.

"Can you do that?" Brenda wondered.

"It's risky, but Ted's the kind of guy who'd go for it."

Ted had taken a long lead off third base, and as the pitcher got ready to throw he leaned his body toward home plate. But the pitcher wasn't taking any chances, and he fired the ball to third while Ted wasn't watching. He dove back to the base, touching it with outstretched fingers. But he was too late. The third baseman tagged him out easily.

The boys booed him good-naturedly, but Chris wished they would be quiet. She could see the disappointment on Ted's face harden into disgust as Terry Detroit yelled, "Sloppy, Mason."

A little while later Ted jogged out into left field. The boys cheered him on, which Ted acknowledged by waving his glove in the air. "Don't egg him on," Chris warned. "It just makes him cocky."

"Are you kidding? He loves it," Brad said. "It's good for his morale."

"But these are tryouts. It's not like he's already made the team," she explained. "He can't impress the coach if he's clowning around for you guys."

"Lighten up," Brad said. "Ted's a natural.

There's no way he's not going to make the team."

"He's right," Woody agreed. Turning to the field, he shouted, "Go for it, Ted."

"Listen, Chris, I hear you've got some competition for the Barnes job," Peter said.

Chris didn't like being reminded. She gave Peter a level gaze. "I know."

"Don't tell me. It's Laurie Bennington," Brenda said.

"Can't be," Phoebe said, shaking her head. "She's definitely going to Europe this summer. So who is it, Peter?"

"Geraldine Gomez. She was talking about it in government class today. She thinks she's in because her uncle's a state senator or some big deal in politics."

"Don't worry, Chris," Brenda said reassuringly. "That's the only thing Geraldine's got going for her."

"But it may be enough," Chris fretted.

"I'm still naive enough to believe that merit does not go unrewarded in this world," Phoebe said. "They wouldn't be setting you up for another interview if they weren't seriously considering you. Those people have got a zillion other things to do than play games with a teenager."

"I hope you're right." Chris's attention returned to the field as a boy hit a fly ball in Ted's direction. It fell to the grass before Ted could reach it. He threw it cleanly back into the infield before too much damage had been done.

The next ball hit the top of Ted's glove and bounced over his head. Chris could barely stand to watch as Ted turned to chase the ball, giving the runners plenty of time to circle the bases.

Peter sat up in time to see the play. "Well, I'll tell you one thing — he's no Reggie Jackson," he commented before lying down again.

"Are you kidding? He's not even a Jake Arkatov," Brad said referring to Kennedy's third-string outfielder. Brad pinched his nose and waved his other hand in the air.

"I've had enough of you guys," Chris declared, standing up.

Brad grabbed her arm. "What's happened to our level-headed Chris? I've never seen you steamed up like this before."

"Well, I've just seen a side of you I've never noticed before either," she spat out. "And I don't like it."

"Aw, come on, Chris. You're in the midst of friends. Can't you take a joke?"

"Sure I can. But where's your sense of decency? That's your friend falling on his face out there," she countered.

"But we're just kidding around."

Brenda had heard enough. "Stop, Brad," she pleaded. "The joke's over when everybody stops laughing."

"Hey, why am I the villain all of a sudden?"

"You're not," Brenda said, giving him a little hug. "I just want you to try to be more sensitive to Chris's feelings."

"So now I'm insensitive, too?" Brad asked.

Scratching the back of his neck, he sighed. "What's a guy to do?"

"Put on a muzzle," Phoebe said. "I remember Sasha giving one to Chris when she won the election. I bet it'll fit you, too."

The comment appeared to ease the tension in the air. "I don't know about you jerks, but I came here to watch these guys play," Phoebe continued. "Anyone care to join me?"

The practice ended before Ted had a chance to redeem himself. No more balls came his way in the field, and he never returned to the plate.

A long hour later Chris and Ted met Brad and Brenda at Mario's, Rose Hill's most popular pizzeria. They sat at Chris's favorite table, a red vinyl booth in the back corner; on the adjacent wall was a picture of a Venetian gondolier that reminded her of a paint-by-the-numbers canvas she had done when she was ten.

Two pizzas, including one with everything, lay half-eaten in front of them. "This is just what I needed after a hard workout," Ted commented, patting his stomach.

"When did you have one?" Brad asked, with a chuckle. "Certainly not this afternoon."

Chris could feel her cheeks flush as she glared across the table. "I'd like to see you play as well," she challenged.

"Nobody can play like old Teddy boy here," Brad joked.

"Yeah, you'd probably be a lot worse," Chris said.

"Hey, cool it, Chris," Ted said good-naturedly.

"It's only a game." When Chris looked up at Ted, though, his eyes told her this baseball league meant more to him than he would admit.

"Anyone for pepperoni?" Brenda asked.

The two couples took separate cars home. Ted was unusually quiet, focusing all his attention on the road ahead of them. He didn't even bother to turn on the radio.

Chris was lost in her own thoughts. Her eyes rested on a small rip at the front corner of Ted's convertible top. "Are you going to get that hole fixed?" she asked.

Ted followed her eyes. "One of these days."

"If I were you, I wouldn't wait. Next time it rains the car's going to get soaked."

"No, it won't. It's just a little rip."

"Why put it off?"

"I'm not putting it off. I just hadn't thought about it till you brought it up. But if you're so stuck on fixing it, why don't you do it yourself?" His voice was beginning to rise.

Chris had not meant to start an argument. "Why in the world are we getting so worked up over a dumb convertible top?" she asked aloud. "I guess I'm just upset about the way the guys ragged you today. They had no right," she declared, folding her arms across her chest.

Ted forced a smile. "Don't be mad at them. A six-year-old could have snagged that ball I dropped."

"Don't punish yourself, Ted. It's only your second day out."

"Yeah, but I'm running out of chances to

54

show them what I can really do. I may end up playing in the A division with Walt the way things are going."

Chris fiddled with the top button of her shirt. It was a nervous habit she had whenever she was unsure about raising a point — like now. "There's something I think I could help with, if you want," she offered. "I noticed something when you ran around the bases. You looked a little winded, like you were out of breath or something. Maybe you need to start running — the way you do during football season."

Ted sighed. "It's easy to do it then with Coach Marshall breathing down my neck. But on my own — I mean, my self-discipline leaves a lot to be desired."

Chris sat up straighter in her seat. "What you need, my dear, is another coach. Like me." She thumped herself on the chest and smiled.

"You?" he chuckled.

"Don't laugh. I'm serious," Chris cried. "I can give you all the encouragement you need. And we could have fun at the same time."

Ted looked at her long and hard. "Okay," he said finally, "but only under one condition — that you push me hard, and not let me give up when I complain. You think you're up to that?"

She nodded. "I'll prove it. I'll go jogging with you tomorrow morning." She looked down at her middle, which was nowhere near as taut as she'd like. "I need to shape up, too, if I'm going to fit into one of those little bikinis you seem to like so much."

He titled his head. "I thought you were swapping your tanning mat for a filing cabinet this summer."

"'But we're still going to have time for *some* fun in the sun. Besides, I haven't gotten that job yet. Now that I know about my competition, I'm afraid maybe I won't."

"Hey, what's the worst that could happen?" Ted laughed. "You won't get your job, I'll get cut from the team, and we'll have to spend the entire summer lying side by side at the pool, soaking up the rays and getting glorious tans."

"Oh, Ted," Chris said, "of course you'll make the team. But whatever you end up doing is all right with me — as long as you save some time for a long-legged blonde — "

Ted laughed. "Some coach. You've already forgotten our conditioning program. I'll see you at least once a day. Starting tomorrow. Seven A.M. in front of your house. Will you be ready?"

Chris groaned. "It was my idea. I'll be there."

Chapter 7

Ted knocked on Chris's front door at five minutes to seven the next day. He'd jogged the two miles from his house, and wet patches were already beginning to show through his sleeveless blue sweat shirt. "Hi, Chris," he said, panting, when she opened the door a moment later. "You ready to — " He stopped when he noticed her clothes. "That's not a running outfit!"

Chris was wearing a yellow-and-black polka-dotted shirtwaist dress. Her black-stockinged feet were still shoeless. "I know," she said, somewhat apologetically. "This is what I'm wearing to school today."

"You look good enough to kiss," he said. Eyes twinkling and alert from his run, he stepped inside and swooped Chris up in his arms.

With his damp hair catching the glow of the early morning sun Ted looked more appealing than ever to her. She kissed him tenderly, the salty taste of his sweat mixing with her toothpaste-fresh mouth.

When they parted, Ted leaned against the door, smiling. "Okay, Hot Lips, go upstairs and change. I'll wait down here for you."

Chris leaned against the bannister and frowned. "I can't make it," she said. "Last night when I got home there was a package from Congressman Barnes's office waiting for me. Inside was a bunch of forms I was supposed to fill out and get back to them this afternoon — some stupid government things."

"So why didn't you do them last night?"

"I did. But that didn't leave me time to finish my homework. I'm doing that now."

Ted furrowed his brow. "If you knew this last night, how come you didn't call and tell me you couldn't run with me?"

Chris smiled. "I know you," she told him.

"Now what's that supposed to mean?" Ted put his hands on his hips.

"If I'd canceled out, you'd have lost your incentive to run this morning. You'd have come up with some kind of excuse, and not run at all. I'm right, aren't I?"

Ted looked down at his sneakered feet. "Yeah, I guess you're right," he whispered. "I'd have slept in."

Chris stood up and, mimicking a move she'd seen Ted's coach make a hundred times, she put an arm on his shoulder. "I'd say you're ready for the jog back to your house," she said in her best coachlike manner. "That's about four miles round trip — not bad for your first day of roadwork. Tomorrow you'll do five."

"What am I getting myself into?" Ted moaned.

"Shape." Chris smiled. "I'll see you at lunch." After giving his nose a kiss, she closed the door gently. Chris knew she was being tough on him, but it was exactly what he needed.

Chris was pacing back and forth in her bedroom when her stepsister knocked on her door.

Without waiting for an answer, Brenda stepped in. "Hey, what's going on in here? I was cleaning up the dinner dishes and from downstairs, it sounded like a stampede of bulls up here."

"It's just me, trying to get my frustrations out. This has been a lousy day."

"Let's see," Brenda said, plopping down on Chris's neatly made bed. "You're as popular, smart, and pretty today as you were yesterday. You've got a neat boyfriend, and the best family in the world, and you're about to get a great summer job. I can see why you're miserable."

Chris gave a small smile. "I guess things are never as bad as they seem. Can we talk?"

Brenda checked her watch. "I'm supposed to be at Brad's now — he says he's got something fun planned."

"I won't keep you," Chris said. She motioned for her to leave.

Brenda shook her head. "No, I always have time for a sisterly chat. What's up?"

"For one thing, that great summer job you just

mentioned. I went to the district office this afternoon and ran into a real idiot of a lady. I have a feeling she might lose all my forms."

"And what if she does?"

Chris hopped up to perch on her desk. "She'll ruin my chances. I'll never get that job."

"And what if you don't?"

"I'll feel miserable."

Brenda rested her chin on her fist, thinking. Chris thought she looked a little like the Rodin sculpture in her art history textbook. "Why?"

"Because I want that job. You know that, Brenda."

"I know. But you've managed to live the rest of your life up till now without it."

Chris sat intently pulling at the frayed edges of her cut-offs removing the strings that were the longest. "It's a great chance to learn how the political system works, the kinds of things books never tell you about."

"But it's not the only place you can do that," Brenda countered. "I'll bet you can get a volunteer job with anyone else if this thing doesn't pan out. You're not in it for the money anyway."

Chris looked at her stepsister as if a veil had been lifted from her eyes. "Now why didn't I think of that?" she wondered aloud. "Sure, working for a congressman would be my first choice, but the mayor's or state senator's office wouldn't be bad either. Brenda, do you think there's a way I can get a common-sense transplant from you?"

Brenda giggled. "You've got a lot more than you give yourself credit for — like the way you made Ted work out this morning, for instance. Pure genius."

"Yeah, Ted — my other worry." Chris sighed. "He's supposed to come over as soon as the tryouts are over."

"Chris, Ted's here to see you." Mrs. Austin shouted up the stairs.

Chris froze momentarily. A sixth sense made her wary about running down right away as she always did. She looked at Brenda.

"I might as well go down with you," Brenda said. "I'm on my way out anyway."

Chris's intuition was confirmed the moment she saw Ted standing, eyes toward the floor, near the coat rack. She was afraid to ask what was wrong, but before there were any awkward pauses Ted blurted out the news. "I didn't make it," he said.

The last thing Ted needed was to see another unhappy face. Chris forced a smile and said, "I don't mind if you're not wearing a Yankee uniform this summer. I think the Reds' uniforms are cuter anyway." She linked her arm through his and walked him into the living room.

Ted turned to Brenda, who was still standing near the door. "Come on in, Brenda. I'm not going to explode. It's just baseball, after all," he said as though he were trying to convince himself. He took in a deep breath. "I didn't make the Reds either," he said as he sat down on the Austins' large sofa.

"But that's impossible," Chris said indignantly. "You're such a good athlete."

"I wasn't good enough," Ted said, sounding as if he couldn't believe it either. "The coach slotted me for the Ramblers."

"Who are they?" Chris asked.

"An A-division team."

Chris tried not to show her surprise.

"I never thought I'd wind up so low," Ted went on. "I'm actually on a team with Walt Weston."

"Hey," Brenda said, "like you said, 'it's only a game.' The Ramblers, or whatever they're called, play with the same balls and bats that the Yankees do."

"The equipment isn't what makes the difference, Brenda," Ted said. "Terry Detroit made the Yankees. So did all of the Kennedy varsity. You don't understand how embarrassing it is to be in the A division when those guys are playing triple-A."

"How locked in are these teams, Ted?" Chris wondered.

"What do you mean?"

"Is it like pro ball, where guys can get moved around according to their ability?"

"If you mean, can Terry be sent down to the Ramblers, the answer is no. But could I move up? I just don't know."

"You ought to find out. I'm speaking to you now as your coach and your girl friend. Think of your being named to the Ramblers not as a slap in the face but as a kick in the pants. It's the kind of incentive that'll make you work really hard at becoming a good ball player."

"I'll find out tomorrow," Ted said. "I'd do anything to be able to face Terry on the same level again. Do you know what he did when my name was called out? He *laughed*, Chris."

Chris felt her eyes tear over, picturing the sight. It just wasn't fair. She put her arm around Ted's shoulder, her head resting against his.

Just then the phone rang. Chris was closest to the living room extension and picked it up. "Oh, hi, Brad," she said. "Yes, she's here." Cupping her hand over the mouthpiece, she whispered, "It's Brad."

Brenda's mouth flew wide open. "I was supposed to be there already!" She grabbed the phone, feeling guilty. "I had an emergency," she told him. Pulling the extension as far away from Chris and Ted as she could, she turned her back to them and whispered, "I couldn't leave. Chris had some things she needed to talk about." She hoped she hadn't made the exaggeration too obvious. Seeing Ted hurting over the baseball team made her react the same way she did when she saw a new person at Garfield House. She didn't want to leave until she knew he was all right. "I'm leaving right now, okay?"

"Sure," Brad said. "I'll be here." But Brenda noticed a hesitation in his voice.

Chapter
8

Brenda walked into the sub shop the following day after school and thought she noticed a familiar dark blond head bent over a menu at a table near the back of the popular hangout. She eased her way through the Friday afternoon crowd, over to the table, and pulled down the menu. "I thought it was you, Ted. Hiding behind a menu isn't going to make you invisible, you know."

"I wasn't hiding," he protested, dropping the menu onto the formica-topped table. Raising his voice so he could be heard over the background music, he continued, "I was trying to decide whether to have my usual cheeseburger and fries or go for something less fattening, like a tuna salad."

Brenda sat down in the empty chair opposite

him, facing the front entrance. "I didn't know you were into nutrition."

"I'm not really," Ted said, shrugging, "but Chris was playing coach during lunch and I'm trying not to break training."

Brenda thought she heard some of the evening's unhappiness lingering in Ted's voice. His shoulders definitely lacked their usual proud quarterback's posture. "It sounds like there's more to it than you're telling," she said. "Do you want to talk about it?"

Ted looked at her and smiled thinly. "How many hours can you spare?"

"That heavy, huh," Brenda said. She looped her black shoulder bag over the back of the chair. "I'm supposed to meet Brad here. He had to run an errand for his mother, but he said he wouldn't be long. Until then, I'm all yours."

Turning around, Ted craned his neck to get a good look at the front door. But the place was packed with so many Kennedy students celebrating the start of the weekend that it was impossible to see past the take-out area in the front. "Chris is getting her hair trimmed. She said she was going home after that, so I guess we can talk now.

"Chris had a fit when she saw me carrying two pieces of cake on my lunch tray. As soon as I sat down she yanked one of the plates from the tray, saying all those empty calories were bad for me. It didn't help that Sasha was there. She started in on all the chemicals and additives they put in commercial cakes."

65

"I can hear it all now," Brenda said, rolling her eyes.

Ted continued, "I still wanted that second piece, though, so I grabbed hold of the plate. It was like a tug-of-war, Chris pulling from one side, me the other. Finally, she let go, but I was still pulling so the cake went flying off the plate — smack onto the ground. A total waste."

"Would you like me to order you a piece now?" Brenda asked, reaching for the menu. Though her sympathies were usually with her stepsister, she knew the side of Chris Ted had seen — the totally controlled person who sometimes forgot it wasn't quite so easy for everyone else.

"No," he said. "We had a long talk after that. Chris felt bad about trashing the cake. She said she'd only been acting as my coach. She feels the better I eat the stronger I'll be, and the stronger I am the better I'll play and so on. Even I can see there's some sense in that."

"Being a good ball player means that much to you?"

"You bet," he said. "Do you know Seth Amey and George Yarnell? They're two of the varsity starters who'll be playing on the Yankees. They're in my first-period class, and when I walked in this morning I saw a look in their eyes I didn't like. It was as if they were saying to me, 'You're not in our league, Mason. You don't rate anymore.' "

"I think you're exaggerating, Ted," Brenda scoffed.

He went on as if he hadn't heard her. "Before

long everybody on the team's going to think I'm a loser. I can't go through the whole summer with that hanging over me. Sure, I'll get to show my stuff during football season, but I can't wait that long. I've got to move up to the triple-A or else."

Just then the waitress came over. "Have you decided what you want?" Her pencil was poised over her order pad.

"I'll have an iced tea," Brenda said. "Ted?"

He looked at the menu one last time. "A tuna sub," he told the waitress.

She still wasn't convinced he had any reason to change his eating habits. "Aren't you making too much out of this, Ted? Changing your whole life just because of a game?"

"This has never happened to me before," Ted protested. "All my life I've always been on the best teams. Now they're telling me I'm not good enough. It's pretty hard to take."

"In other words, you're feeling rejected."

"Well, I don't know if I'd call it that — "

"It's the truth. Listen, Ted, when it comes to rejection I'm a real pro. Sometimes I think I ought to teach a class called How to Handle Rejection with Style." She smiled. "Rule number one is: Never ever take anything too seriously."

"That's easy for you to say. You've got your life straightened out now," Ted said dejectedly.

Brenda sat up. Ted was such a happy-go-lucky guy it really hurt her to see him taking this so hard.

"Listen, Ted, if I've learned anything it's this:

Don't waste your time worrying about what other people think of you. They only end up seeing what they want to see anyway." She pointed a finger at him. "Do you know why everyone looks up to you as a great quarterback?"

"Because they like football?" He raised his eyebrows to show he didn't take the question seriously.

But Brenda did. "It's because you *act* like a great quarterback. I've noticed how you walk through the school halls. Your head is high and there's always a smile on your face. That's confidence, Ted, and this whole baseball episode is messing yours up."

"I don't know how to deal with it," he grumbled darkly.

Ted looked so vulnerable Brenda wanted to help him somehow. She remembered something Tony Martinez, the director of Garfield House, once did with her. She leaned across the table. "Take a look at my eyes," she demanded. "Be honest. What do you see?"

Ted stared at her for a moment. "Brown pupils with tiny yellow flecks — hey, I didn't know they were there," he added with a smile.

"But do you think that I think you're a loser?"

Ted paused before answering, "No. But Chris does."

Brenda sat back. "I don't believe that for a minute."

"She says she doesn't, but she acts like she does. I'm sure all of her pushing me to get in shape has a lot to do with her not wanting to hang out with a loser."

The waitress brought their food to the table. Ted took one look at his plate and pushed it away. "Suddenly I'm not so hungry," he said.

Brenda stared at it. "Mind if I take a bite? I was going to wait till Brad got here, but I'm starved."

"Help yourself." He pushed the plate to her side of the table and continued, "Chris has never settled for second-best. That's what's driving me crazy." He lowered his voice and leaned closer to Brenda. "I'd never tell this to anyone else, but I know I can trust you. I'd have quit the baseball league if it hadn't been for her. The only thing that's keeping me in now is knowing how disgusted with me she'd be if I gave up. The only thing she hates more than a loser is a quitter."

"I don't think she hates either," Brenda said. "Chris has only been trying to act in your best interest."

"That's because she's really counting on me doing well this summer. All I have to do is improve my play enough to get on the Yankees. Once I've done that I can relax and start enjoying the game again."

Brenda shook her head. "Ted, I can't speak for Chris, although I usually have a pretty good idea what she's thinking. But I can speak for myself." She reached across the table and took his hand. "I don't think you're a loser or a quitter. In fact,

I think you're pretty great. And I wouldn't change my mind if you quit the baseball team *and* the football team."

For a few seconds, Ted looked down at the table. Then he stared directly into Brenda's eyes. "I never knew you thought about me at all, Brenda. I — " He paused, fumbling for words. "You've been a big help." He looked back down at the table. He seemed to be eyeing the sandwich.

Brenda pushed the plate over, giggling. "You look a little hungry, Ted. Have a sub sandwich."

As she reached for her drink she saw Brad coming toward the table, a brown paper bag in his hand. His jawline was tense, and Brenda wondered what had happened to make him so upset. He looked as if he were about to say something to her, but apparently he had second thoughts as soon as he arrived at the table.

Brenda saw him gulp. "Uh, hi, there," he said. His face relaxed considerably. "Hi, Ted," he added. "You had me going there for a second. I saw Brenda sitting with a guy and started to get a little nervous. But it's only you."

Ted laughed loudly. "No, you were right the first time, Davidson. I'm sitting here in the busiest place in Rose Hill hitting on my girl friend's sister and best friend's girl friend." They all three laughed at that.

"You two are looking at the happiest guy in Maryland," Brad announced as he sat next to Brenda.

"Are you going to tell us why or sit there all

70

day with that goofy smile on your face?" Brenda asked.

"You'd be smiling, too, if you just found out you were getting a brand-new car for graduation."

"Brad, that's fantasic," Brenda said, hugging him around the neck.

"What are you doing tomorrow night, Brenda?" Brad asked.

"I thought we had a date."

"And you, Ted?" he asked.

"Probably a movie with Chris."

"No, you're not. You're all coming over to my house. I'm in the mood to celebrate."

"You know I'm always up for a party," Brenda said.

"I've got an idea for something different. My mother told me about a party she threw when she was in high school."

"What'd they do, sit around and wash the floor?" Brenda deadpanned. Mrs. Davidson was known for her meticulously clean house.

"Very funny," he retorted. "No, it'll be a regular party. The only difference is that in order to get in, everybody's got to bring something that reminds them of their favorite person at Kennedy — boyfriend, girl friend, best friend, whatever. They'll all get put in a big can. Midway through the party we'll make a game out of it by trying to figure out who brought what. It'll be a good way to sort of replay the year."

"Sounds pretty corny to me," Ted said.

"That's the whole point," Brad said. "The

71

cornier it is, the more fun it'll be. I was trying to think what some people would bring. Woody might bring an éclair for Kim, Chris might bring a football for you, Peter might bring a door-knob — "

"What on earth for?" Brenda asked.

"He and Monica finally got together when they got locked in the WKND record library by a broken doorknob, remember?" Brad laughed. "I'm telling everyone to be as weird and creative about this as they'd like. My contribution is right here." He held the paper bag. "But you're going to have to wait until the party to see what it is."

"Oh, I don't know how I'll ever stand the wait," Brenda said dryly.

"Come on," he nudged her, "it's going to be fun. My mom said the things her friends brought made it a party she's never forgotten."

"But it's tomorrow night. That's not a lot of time to come up with something," Ted complained.

"Come on, Ted. You won't need twenty-four hours to get an inspiration."

Brenda had an idea. "Would I be able to take the thing back home with me after the party?"

"Sure, if you want." Brad said.

She smiled mysteriously. "Then I know exactly what I'm going to bring."

"What?" Brad demanded.

"Uh-uh," she said, shaking her head. "Telling you would take all the fun out of it. You're just going to have to wait."

Chapter 9

"There. Perfect," Brenda said as she pulled the Davidsons' wrought-iron love seat to the edge of the patio. "Plenty of room to dance, and plenty of spots to sit and talk." She plopped down on the seat and patted the spot next to her.

"Come reward me for my troubles."

Brad sat down next to her and stroked her thick dark hair. "Brenda, you look beautiful tonight. Why don't we just send everybody else away and make this a private event?" As if on cue, Woody Webster popped his head through the patio's sliding glass door. "The party can start. I'm here," he announced.

"You mean the food is here," Kim said. She was right behind him carrying a serving tray in her arms. "Brad, could you help us unload the rest?"

Brenda busied herself setting up the tray Kim brought in, checking the door every few seconds for her friends, pleased when Chris finally came in with Ted and Sasha.

By this time Brad had come back and turned on the stereo, filling the patio with dance music.

Brad pulled Brenda out to the middle of the room. "Let's dance," he said. "We'll end up with a bunch of stiffs lining the walls if we don't show 'em how to do it."

"If you're the teacher, we're in trouble," Brenda said with a giggle. Brad's dancing was about as graceful as a mule on roller skates.

"I can't think of anyone's toes I'd rather step on," he joked back.

Brenda smiled. Brad glanced around at the rapidly filling dance floor. "Hey, I could get a job as the Pied Piper of Hamelin. See, everybody's joined us."

Within minutes, two dozen partygoers had drifted in. Since the night was warm, most of them were dressed casually in shorts, T-shirts, topsiders, or tennis shoes. Woody got his vote for most colorful outfit: red-and-white checked shorts topped by a bold blue-and-yellow striped shirt, and of course, the famous red suspenders. Laurie Bennington wore a patterned silk romper Brenda thought she had seen in a recent issue of *Vogue.*

With each beat of the music the patio swelled with dancers, leaving not much room to do more than sway back and forth in place.

For Brenda, the party was a relaxing contrast

to the life she had confronted at Garfield House that afternoon. She would have been content to dance like that for hours, with her boyfriend smiling lovingly at her, but after the song was over, the deejay came back on the air with commercials, and all the dancing stopped.

A collective groan filled the air as the couples drifted away. Brad and Brenda leaned against the refreshment table. Peter and Monica followed right behind them.

"Hey, Brad, I thought maybe you could use this," Peter said. He reached into the front pocket of his brown cargo pants and tossed a small box into Brad's lap, momentarily startling him.

"What is it?" Brad asked. "The mementos are supposed to go in that garbage pail."

"This is our donation to good times tonight," Monica explained.

Brad opened the box. Inside was a cassette labeled *Party Music*. "It's just what the doctor ordered," he said.

"Hey, watch it, Davidson," Peter remarked. "You've got about another ten years or so before you're entitled to put that M.D. after your name."

"Ten years! Don't remind me," Brad said, laughing. "I'll go put on the tape. These dumb commercials are getting on my nerves, too."

Brenda stayed behind, taking the time to catch her breath and survey the scene. Kim was setting up more trays of bite-sized nibbles. Woody was right behind her, sampling each one. Brenda giggled to herself. Kim seemed unaware that

Woody was right behind her, instantly undoing her painstaking arrangements.

Brad motioned for Brenda to join him, but as she began to squeeze through the crowd she noticed he'd gotten caught up in a conversation with some seniors. She felt awkward in such situations recently, having little to say about caps, and gowns, and diplomas. So she drifted over to where Chris and Ted were standing with Sasha. "Have you tried Sasha's pizza?" Chris asked. "It's delish."

Brenda noticed the remnants of a crust in Chris's napkin. "Not yet. Where is it?"

"I left it in the kitchen, where it'll stay warm," Sasha said. "I'm taking orders. Brad's mother doesn't want everyone tromping in there."

"I know," Brenda said, "she told me. Sure, I'll take a slice."

"Where's Phoebe?" she asked as Sasha headed for the kitchen.

"She said she might stop by later. She had her singing lesson this afternoon, and after that she was supposed to listen to some of Michael's new songs." Chris sighed. "I'd like to see her either get involved with him or really start looking for a new boyfriend. She hasn't had a date since she and Griffin broke up."

"Phoebe seems pretty happy with herself these days, though. There is such a thing as life without boys, you know." Brenda sighed. "I wish other people's problems were as easy to solve as hers."

Chris read her thoughts. "Tough day at Garfield House?"

Brenda nodded. "I spent a lot of time with this one girl, Billie, whose parents are going through a big divorce. They've been putting a lot of pressure on her to take sides. I tried to convince her to hang in there, but all she wants to do is run away."

"I can understand the feeling," Ted sympathized.

"But it's a terrible idea," Brenda said, looking hard at him. "As bad as things are for her at home, it's bound to be much worse for her on the outside."

As Sasha handed Brenda her pizza, Chris spotted her best friend across the crowd. "There's Phoebe. I'm going to go talk to her for a minute. She said she wanted to check out my new haircut."

Brenda balanced the paper plate in one hand while holding her slice of pizza in the other. She took a bite. "Ow, it's hot," she cried.

"Here, let me get you a soda," Ted said. He dashed to the table and returned momentarily with the drink. "I always say a pizza's not a pizza unless it burns the roof of your mouth."

Brenda downed a long gulp. "It's a shame the best food always has its drawbacks. Chocolate makes me break out, pizza always ends up around my waistline."

"I don't see it there," Ted said.

Brenda took another bite of the pizza, this time

blowing on it before bringing it to her mouth. "So how's baseball going?"

The smile vanished from his face. "Nothing's happening yet. Our official team practice starts Monday afternoon. Until then I'm just getting into shape."

"I know. You must have had some workout with Chris this morning. She was so drenched I thought it was raining."

"That sister of yours is a real slave driver," Ted agreed, wincing. "But I think I've discovered a better way to get in shape. I was watching you with Brad earlier. You're a great dancer. Maybe you can teach me a few moves tonight."

"I'd love to! Brad doesn't really like to dance much, but he humors me."

Ted wrapped his arms playfully around Brenda's waist. "Humors you?" He stared into her eyes. "*I'd* consider it an honor."

Just then Brad turned down the stereo. "Attention, everybody," he shouted. "The main event is about to begin."

Chapter
10

Brad waved his arms to draw everyone's attention. "Hi, folks. To those I haven't had a chance to speak to, I'd like to welcome you to my party. Hope you've all had a chance to taste the goodies Kim and Sasha brought along. As you can see, right here next to me is a pail. I'm picking out a memento right now. Let's see if we can guess who the item represents and who brought it." Brad unwrapped the first piece: a record jacket. "Guesses, anyone?"

At first he was greeted with dead silence. Then Woody looked around and shouted out, "It's a record jacket." His answer was greeted by hoots and giggles. He raised his hands helplessly. "Well, someone had to break the ice for you geeks. I don't know about you, but my guess is — "

"Peter Lacey," a chorus responded. It looked

like Woody's ice-breaker was just what was needed to get the guessing game going.

Brad looked at his friend. "Looks as though you're typecast, Lacey. Have any idea who brought it?"

Peter looked at his girl friend. "You, Monica?"

She nodded. "Notice who's on the cover?"

"How could I miss him — the Boss!" Bruce Springsteen was Peter's favorite. "I hope you took the record out. If it got crushed in that pile, I'll kill you."

Brenda was standing at the back of the room, watching with interest how much Brad was relishing his role as host. Corny or not, the game was holding everyone's attention. Not everyone was as easy to guess as Peter, though. Brenda thought the page of sheet music Brad held up was for Randy Nakamora, who was considered the best pianist Kennedy had ever produced. It turned out to have been for Woody. Kim had brought it because it was the music to their favorite song. Brenda hadn't even been able to guess that the red jellybeans Ted had brought were a reminder of the time Chris had left a bag of them on the seat of the car, where they melted under the hot sun.

Brad had gone through most of the items when he pulled out a green-and-white knit ski cap. Brenda felt a funny sensation in her stomach as she realized it was Brad's memento of her, a reminder of the skiing trip where they first really got to know each other. She didn't say a word, letting Chris and Ted be the ones to figure it out. Then, when Brad confirmed their guesses she rushed up to the front and put the cap on. Since it actually was Brad's it was too big for her head, and when she put it on it came down over her eyes. But resolutely she rolled up the bottom of it and perched it atop her head, holding it in place with her sunglasses. She told Brad she'd wear it the rest of the evening.

Next Brad pulled out a gold locket. He looked at it closely. The mementos were supposed to be inexpensive trifles, but this was the real thing. He looked at the tag. His blank expression gave away his surprise. "Any guesses?" he asked.

"There aren't too many people left," Kim said. "I'll take a guess and say Sasha."

"No," Brad said. "I'll give you a hint. It's someone who's already been mentioned."

Ted peered closely at the locket, then whispered, "I thought it looked familiar." Much louder he announced, "I know who. Chris Austin . . . and it's from Brenda."

Chris smiled at her stepsister. "Thanks. This means a lot to me," she whispered.

"Me, too," Brenda said. Chris had given her the locket for Christmas. "I know Brad meant this as a gag, but if it hadn't been for you I wouldn't have had anything at Kennedy. Not Brad. Not my friends. Not my happiness." Despite herself, she started to cry. Pulling her head closer to Chris, she whispered, "I love you, Sis."

Chris threw her arms around her stepsister. "Me, too," she said. For a brief moment the two girls held each other tightly. Then Chris added,

"But I think I ought to tell you, I chose something for Ted."

"I'm not surprised," Brenda said. "I sort of expected you would."

Brad had been watching the exchange. Silently, he handed the locket to Chris as she stepped forward, then he picked up the next item, a wind-up plastic football player.

Before he said anything, Wood shouted, "It's Ted."

Chris blurted out, "He's right. I got it."

She was greeted with boos. "You didn't give us a chance to figure that out," Sasha said. "Not that it would have taken us very long."

Brenda stood with Chris and Ted as Brad continued to emcee the game. She couldn't help noticing that his enthusiasm had dwindled after he'd pulled out the locket.

"At last," Brenda said as Brad turned the dance tape on again. "If you'll excuse me, I've got to find my dancing partner. I'll catch up with you later." Ted looked as if he was about to protest, but she didn't give him time.

Brenda moved through the crowd toward Brad, but when she caught up with him he was talking to another senior, Gayle Tuttle, the girl he would be walking with on graduation night. Overhearing him say the words "graduation day" sent her back to the snack table. Over baby hot dogs she ended up talking to Peter about the new Talking Heads album.

She finally rejoined Brad after she saw Gayle drift off toward the backyard.

"Ah, my wandering gypsy has returned," Brad said, sounding annoyed.

"Did anyone ever tell you, you sound like a late night movie?" she asked him. "I haven't gone anywhere." She grasped his shoulders and started dancing with him, moving in time to the slow song coming out over the speakers.

"You could have fooled me," Brad said. "It's like you're avoiding me."

"Oh, no," she said. "I just didn't want to cramp your style while you were playing host with the girls — especially when the topic of conversation was the big G."

"I wouldn't have minded."

"But I feel like a fifth wheel when you're talking about who's going to be walking down the aisle with whom and all that stuff."

"I didn't know I'd turned into such a bore," he replied stiffly.

"Oh, come on, don't take it that way," she said. "Something else is bothering you, I can tell. Do you want to talk about it?"

Brad sighed. "I guess it's silly, but I thought you'd have brought something for me."

Brenda pursed her lips. "You know you're my favorite guy in the world, Brad. But I really believe I'd never have cut it at Kennedy if it hadn't been for Chris. You can understand that, can't you?"

"When you put it that way. . . ."

Brenda took his chin and turned his face so that he was looking into her eyes. "Brad Davidson, you're a dope if you can't see how special

83

you are to me. You don't need a silly gag gift to prove it, now, do you?"

"No, but — "

"But what?"

Brad looked down at the floor. "Nobody else picked me either."

"Oh, Brad," she said softly, feeling his pain. Brenda put her arms around him and held him close to her, hoping this moment of togetherness could make up for his disappointment.

Just then Ted tapped on Brad's shoulder. "Let's switch Austins," he suggested.

"Sure, I don't mind," Brad said.

Brenda didn't let go of him. "Are you sure?" she whispered in his ear. Ted's timing couldn't have been worse.

"Sure, go ahead. I'll be fine," Brad said.

"Nice to see you again, Ted," she said.

"Chris and I just thought it was time for a change of pace," Ted said.

Brenda looked at Chris and wondered how much say her stepsister really had in the matter. "So, are you enjoying the party?"

"I am now," he said. A slow Lionel Richie song began to play, and Ted wrapped his muscular arms tightly around Brenda.

"Have you and Chris had a chance to talk tonight?" Brenda asked.

"Not really. But things are okay, I guess. I've been feeling a lot more relaxed about everything ever since we talked at the sub shop."

"I'm glad, Ted. I've got to admit, it's nice to feel needed. Brad's got his act so completely together that I sometimes wonder, even though I know he cares about me, if he really needs me."

"Well, right now, Brenda, I need you, and you're helping me a lot." Ted was nearly a foot taller than Brenda, and as the conversation ended, he pulled her closer, resting his chin on top of her head. She searched the dance floor for Chris and Brad, but they had left. She saw them at last through the kitchen window, talking to Mrs. Davidson with their backs to the dance floor.

As the music ended, Ted kept one arm around Brenda. With the other, he lifted her chin toward his face. "Thanks, Bren," he said. Then before Brenda knew what was happening, he leaned down and kissed her softly on the lips.

"Um, you're welcome, Ted," Brenda said when he released her. "I think we should go look for Brad and Chris, don't you?"

"Sure. I think I saw them go toward the house." He looked so relaxed that Brenda was angry at herself for suspecting that his kiss was anything more than friendly gratitude.

Chapter
11

Early Monday morning Chris got a rude awakening. "Chris, wake up. Come on, Ted's waiting for you downstairs."

Groggily, she rolled over, and slowly her father's face came into focus. "T — Ted?" she mumbled.

"Mm-hmm," Mr. Austin replied. "Looks to me as if that fella's ready to do some serious roadwork."

"The workout!" Chris bolted upright, as alert as if she'd been drenched with a bucket of ice water. "What time is it?" She checked her alarm clock. Seven o'clock. Looking closer she saw that the button was set to "alarm off."

Jumping out of bed, Chris quickly ran to her closet. "Tell Ted I'll be right down," she told her father. Under her breath she added, "He's going to kill me!" She continued to rifle through her closet, looking for her robe. She found it and threw it on. Then, still barefoot, she rushed downstairs.

Ted was leaning against the bannister. Chris's heart melted when she saw him, dressed in a brand-new ice-blue sweat suit. The run had made his skin glisten, and he looked anxious to continue. She wondered how she could have been stupid enough not to set the alarm.

She grabbed Ted around the waist, glad her parents were in the kitchen. "Good morning, Ted," she said in as cheerful a voice as she could muster, given her lack of sleep.

"Don't tell me you're running in this!" he said. He tugged playfully at her terry-cloth belt.

"It's the very latest design in athletic gear," she quipped, stepping back to model her outfit for him. "Actually, I overslept this morning. I'm sorry, Ted."

"That's okay. I can wait while you change. It shouldn't take long."

She shook her head. "I don't think I can run. I hardly got any sleep at all. I was up till midnight getting ready for my meeting this afternoon with Mr. Wingate. He wants to talk about my plans for fund raising activities for next year. Brad said he'd help me with that, but I'd forgotten till it was too late to call him, so I sat up and thought up a bunch of things on my own. I fell into my bed and was totally out of it till my dad woke me up."

"So you're not coming with me?"

"Why not stay and have breakfast with me?

You're entitled to a day off." She smiled impishly. "Coach's orders."

"Shouldn't that be my decision?" Ted asked. His eyebrows shot up, the way they did whenever he got angry.

Chris was surprised by the reaction. "Of course, Ted. I didn't mean to sound like I was telling you what to do. I'm just trying to find a way to make it up to you for oversleeping."

"Don't you realize what today is?"

"Monday?" she asked tentatively.

"It's the first day of team practice. I was counting on this run to pump me up for the day — get me psyched for this afternoon."

Chris moved closer again and rubbed her cheek against his. With her finger she lightly drew circles around his ears. "I'm sorry I've ruined your day," she said. "Let me make it up to you. What if I treat you to a movie tonight?"

"Which one?"

"That new one at the Cinema 5?"

Ted smiled. "It's a date," he said. "But only on one condition. That you be my guest for lunch at one of Kennedy High's finest eating establishments."

"The cafeteria? I always said you had impeccable taste in dining, Mason. You know I'll be there." She winked as she smoothed her robe. "And dressed in proper attire, of course."

Chris felt the day's tension drain from her body as she sat next to Ted in the theater. The dim, cavernous room was practically empty on this Monday night. The dark solitude was a perfect atmosphere for her to relax in after what had been a busy day, especially with Ted's reassuring warmth within reach.

Her meeting with Mr. Wingate had lasted much longer than she'd expected. He'd gone over each of her ideas painstakingly, in an effort to determine which ones were feasible. The ideas she'd outlined in detail were the ones he'd set aside as routine, typical, and boring. But there were a few she'd scribbled down late into the night that he'd told her were daring, original, and likely to inspire the students. He'd closed the meeting saying he looked forward to Chris's being president and predicting she would be Kennedy's best one ever. He'd also set up another meeting for later in the week to map out a strategy for the following year.

On her way home, she'd made a special stop at Sasha's house to share the news. Sasha had told her so many times about the power of inspiration, and how she always waited for the right moment to come when ideas literally popped into her head. Chris usually preferred total preparation to ad libbing, but now she thought Sasha might be on to something.

But there was even more good news waiting for her at home. She found a letter from Congressman Barnes's office inviting her for a final interview that Friday afternoon. She'd be meeting the head of the district office, the person who worked directly with the congressman himself. Chris had read the letter several times to make sure she really understood it. It didn't mean she had the job, but she was definitely one step closer. This is it, she told herself excitedly. She had only four days in which to prepare, but she vowed to go into that office primed to sell Chris Austin as she'd never been sold before.

She was dying to tell Ted all this. She was equally curious to find out how his practice had gone. But she hadn't yet gotten the chance. As they drove to the theater, Ted had talked about Brad's party and the hard time Mr. Baylor had given Phoebe in algebra class that day, almost as if they were avoiding some subject he was afraid Chris might bring up.

By the time the movie ended, Chris's nervous energy had dissipated, and she was reluctant to leave the theater. Its cool air was a relief from the still oppressive humidity outside. Ted nudged her gently as the credits began to roll. "It's time to go," he said. "It's over."

Chris smoothed out the front of her pullover shirt, tucking it inside her jeans as she got up from her seat. "I'm in the mood for ice cream," she said. "What about you?"

"What about my diet?" he asked. "I thought I was in training."

"Take the night off," she said.

Ted stared at her, as if he were going to say something. Instead he followed her up the escalator.

The theater was in a large mall at the edge of Rose Hill. The floor above it was dedicated to fast food shops serving a variety of international foods. Chris led Ted to Elliott's Famous Flavors, an ice cream store and Rose Hill institution nestled between the Chinese and Mexican food stands. Remaining at arm's length behind her, Ted walked down the glass counter, surveying the choice of flavors.

Chris stopped short in front of one freezer. "We've got to get that," she said, pointing.

"Baseball nut?" Ted read the flavor. "Give me a break, huh, Chris?"

"But it's in honor of your first day of practice."

"I'm not in the mood for jokes," he said. "I'm getting a plain old strawberry cone."

Chris ordered a baseball nut cone with sprinkles.

Outside the store they began to eat. "You sure you don't want to try this? It's good," Chris said, taking another lick.

"If it has anything to do with baseball, I don't want to get anywhere near it," he growled. He stepped up his pace, and Chris had to jog a little to catch up.

"Hey, what happened today?" Chris asked as she reached his side. "Did you strike out again?"

"And what if I did?" Ted jumped on her words.

Chris could see she'd struck a raw nerve. "Sorry I brought it up. I had no idea. . . ."

"Let's just drop the subject, okay?"

Chris knew better than to coax Ted into talking. She'd try again later after he calmed down.

"Want to hear about my day?" she asked, trying to sound cheery as she took another bite from her cone. Chris took Ted's silence as a yes and continued. "I've got an interview at Barnes's office on Friday," she announced. She'd planned to make it a low-key statement, but she couldn't contain her excitement about the news. "I think this means I'm in," she told him. "That is, if I don't blow it completely."

"Chris Austin would never blow it," Ted mumbled.

Chris felt as if a firecracker had blown up in her head. She hadn't done anything to make him mad, but she sensed that anything she said would get the same reaction. She felt stung by his words.

"Ted, you sure you're all right? Maybe you'd better tell me what happened."

"Nothing."

Chris shrugged. Perhaps if she kept talking as usual he would forget whatever was bothering him and become his natural, easygoing self. "I had a terrific meeting with Mr. Wingate after school. He really liked my fund raising ideas." She grabbed his arm. "My staying up late was sure worth it."

Ted let go of her hand. "Yeah, for you, maybe."

"Look, I told you I was sorry about this morninging. I promise — I'll make it up to you."

"Chris, some things can't be fixed just because you say they will be. You know, you're so used to living in a perfect world, I'm not sure that you can understand someone who doesn't."

This didn't sound like her boyfriend. In the

past Ted had always loved to hear about her accomplishments, but the guy standing next to her was turning on her like a caged tiger. "Ted, what are you talking about?" she cried.

"If you don't know, I can't explain it to you," he growled. That was all he would say. He and Chris walked silently to the car, and he drove her home.

He didn't even kiss her good night.

Tears were already streaming down Chris's face by the time she reached her front door. Overnight it seemed that Ted had changed from a loving guy to someone who only loved dumping on her. She had done everything she could think of to help him get over his disappointment about baseball, and he ended up blaming her for all that was wrong in his life.

She slipped in the door and tiptoed up to her room, careful not to disturb her parents, who were watching TV in the family room. Brenda's door was open, but she was nowhere to be seen.

Chris couldn't remember the last time she'd felt so confused. She wanted to throw herself on her bed and cry her heart out, but she also wanted to rip every picture of Ted off her bedroom bulletin board.

There was only one thing to do. She called Phoebe and filled her in on everything that had happened that day.

"No matter what I said, he took everything out on me," Chris concluded. "So what do I do?"

"Dr. Phoebe says there isss only vun thing to do in a case like ziss," she said, doing her best

93

imitation of Dr. Ruth, the radio psychologist. "Listen to your heart. Vat iss it telling you?"

Chris paused. "It's saying, 'Be patient, this will blow over.' But my mind's saying, 'Murder the jerk.' "

"Don't you think that's pretty drastic?" Phoebe wondered, returning to her regular voice.

"Well, what do you think I should do?" she asked again.

"Truth is, I've never totally understood the chemistry between you two. It's as if you're an unbalanced compound, ready to disintegrate given the right set of circumstances."

"You mean you don't think we belong together?"

"Well, no, it's not that. There's some indefinable force that draws you two together. Be patient. Hang in there. He'll pull out of it. I think — "

"Hold on, Phebe. There's a call on the other line. I'll be right back." Chris pushed the hold button and then took the other call. "Hello?"

"Chris?" Her heart beat faster at the sound of Ted's voice. "Oh, Chris, I owe you a big apology. I acted rotten tonight, and I'm really sorry."

There was a pause on the line as Chris waited for him to continue. When he didn't, she said, "Is that all you've got to say?" Her voice was stiff and very controlled, her defense against totally falling apart.

"What else can I say? I'm — I'm not mad at you."

"Well, maybe I'm mad, Ted. You said some pretty mean things to me."

"It's not you — it's me, Chris," Ted said. "I'm a real jerk."

"I had looked forward to having a good time tonight."

"And I ruined it, I know. Think you can forgive me? Or do I have to crawl over to your house on my hands and knees, throw stones at your window, and cry my heart out first?"

Chris giggled.

"I heard that." he said. In a more serious tone he added, "I'm sorry, Chris. Look, I don't want to talk about what happened today except to say that practice didn't go very well."

"I'm sorry," Chris said, relieved. All her dark imaginings about what was wrong between them disappeared. "All you had to do was tell me that. I understand."

"Good. Then I'll see you tomorrow morning at seven?"

"It's a deal. I'll even be dressed for running this time. Good night." She kissed the phone before taking Phoebe off hold.

"Pheeb, you still there?"

"Ever faithful. While you were gone, I took a shower, polished my nails, finished my homework. . . ."

Chris laughed. "I wasn't gone that long. Besides, it was an important call."

"Ted?"

"Yes. You know that stuff we were just talking about? Forget it. False alarm."

95

"I knew it," Phoebe said triumphantly. "I just knew it."

"So my love life is fine again. I guess the trick is just not to take Ted's grumbling so seriously. In this case, the solution seems to be, the less attention you pay to the problem, the better."

Chapter
12

Brenda was curled up on the sofa, her trigonometry book wedged between her thighs. The TV in the background was tuned to a mindless action series that she didn't really like, except for the energetic music that blasted forth during the car chases. In her left hand she was balancing her notebook. On it, instead of formulas, she had drawn an elaborate pattern of triangles enmeshed in circles and squares. If she stared at it long enough, maybe the complicated picture could inspire her to figure out the answers to the problems in her textbook.

Brenda was worried. Her trigonometry final was still a week and a half away, but it was her first, and it counted for one-third of her grade for the year. As far as she was concerned it was her toughest test. Up until then she'd managed to maintain a B average, thanks in large part to Chris, who seemed to understand the hieroglyphics a lot better than she did.

But Chris couldn't help her now; she was too preoccupied with her own classes, her upcoming job interview, and what she described as Ted's suddenly strange behavior. She had gone to Kim's house to study.

Brenda began to tap her pencil on the pad, in time to the music coming from the TV set. Maybe, she thought, she ought to tap on her head instead, to try to dislodge the formulas from her brain. They had to be in there somewhere, she reasoned. She'd paid such careful attention to Mr. McClure's lectures, writing down what he'd said word for word. But, as had happened all year, once she got home her scribbled class notes never seemed to make much sense.

She stared at the first problem again. She would figure out the answer if it took her all night, she told herself. In one sense that in itself was a victory. As recently as winter, she wouldn't have believed she could ever push her personal problems aside long enough to concentrate on studying.

Forcing herself to bear down, she began to work on the first problem. To her pleasant surprise she came up with the solution before the first commercial came on. She was halfway through solving the second one when she heard a knock on the door.

Mildly nervous, she tiptoed lightly to the door. She hadn't been expecting anyone, and except for the stuffed animals in Chris's room, no one else was home. "Who is it?" she asked, lowering her voice to make it sound more authoritative.

"It's me — Brad. Let me in."

Brenda unlocked the door. "What in the world . . ." she gasped.

Brad turned around in a full circle modeling his blue graduation cap and gown. "What do you think? I just got it this afternoon."

"It looks like a good fit," she said. "But what are you doing here? I thought you were working on your biology term paper tonight."

"I've had it with fish." Brad closed the door with his sneakered foot and sauntered into the living room. He leaned against the back of one of the upholstered chairs. With his black T-shirt showing under the open gown he reminded Brenda a little of a tom cat stretching — or maybe he looked more like the Cheshire cat. He was grinning from ear to ear, like somebody just dying to reveal a secret.

Brenda folded her arms as she followed him into the room. "So you came to see me?"

"Even better than that." He lowered his eyes to her bare feet. "Go put your shoes on."

"No. I like being barefoot."

"Come on, Brenda, please," he asked again. "I'm taking you out."

"In that?"

He chuckled. "Don't worry, I'll take it off, eventually." He reached for her hand. "Let's go."

Backing away, Brenda pursed her lips. "I'd like to, Brad, but I've got tons of homework."

"So what? You can do it in the morning."

"No, I won't have enough time. It's trigonometry, and you know how hard it is for me." Losing ground in the course would get her in deep trouble with her stepfather, who checked her grades as closely as an investor monitoring the New York Stock Exchange.

Brad's smile faded. "You know I don't have enough time either. Two and a half weeks to graduation."

Brenda felt tempted to give in but held her ground. "Do you really think I'd say no if it weren't absolutely necessary?"

"No," he admitted softly, after a long pause. "I've been where you are, too."

Brenda searched for a compromise. "Why don't you stay and watch TV? Maybe by the time this show's over I'll be through with my homework."

Brad turned to the flickering set in the corner. "Hey, I haven't seen this show in ages," he said. "Okay, I'll go help myself to a snack in the kitchen. Where are your folks?"

"Dad's working. Mom's playing bridge at a friend's." And to answer his unasked question she added, "Chris is out, too. We've got the house to ourselves."

Brad took off his cap and gown and draped them over a chair. "Hmm, this could turn out even better than my original plan," Brad said, giving her an exaggerated leer.

They both laughed.

With Brad in the room it was harder for

Brenda to concentrate on her work. Silently she cursed herself for not having paid more attention to math in grade school. Now she realized why it was important. She moved over to one of the chairs, which blocked her view of Brad. If she concentrated hard, maybe she could pretend he wasn't there. Such was the price of scholarship.

After the TV show was over Brad went into the kitchen and spooned himself out a dish of ice cream. When he came back he flicked through the channels, finally stopping at an Orioles' baseball game. Still working, Brenda sneaked a peek at him. She wished he'd gotten some ice cream for her, too. But she wasn't mad; she knew he hadn't wanted to disturb her by asking.

It was close to ten when she finally finished. "Phew! I'm done," she announced, closing her notebook with a triumphant thud.

When Brad didn't react she rose from the chair and had to stifle a giggle when she reached the sofa. Brad was sound asleep.

Gently, she roused him and sent him home. "We'll go out tomorrow night," she told him. "I promise."

But the following morning her mother reminded her about the dentist appointment she had scheduled early that evening. Brenda ended up having two cavities filled and came home with a mouth so numb from the novocaine that she canceled the date. She couldn't face going out with chipmunk cheeks and a mouth that felt like lead. Brad told her he understood, and they made another date for the following night.

* * *

At seven-ten Thursday evening, the sky was already darkening as Brenda got off the bus from Washington and ran the three blocks to her house at full speed. She was glad she'd worn running shoes. Tony Martinez, the head peer counselor at Garfield House, had called her at school that morning with an emergency. The girl she'd talked into returning to her mother's house had come back and refused to talk to anyone except Brenda. Brenda had agreed readily to rush into town, hopping on a bus as soon as her last class had let out.

Now, exhausted, she dragged herself up the stairs to her room to get dressed for her date with Brad. She chose an oversized yellow T-shirt to wear over her jeans, hopeful that the bright color would help lighten her mood. Her confrontation with the girl had left her drained.

While she was freshening up her makeup, her stepsister knocked on her door. "Come on in, Chris," she called.

"I'm glad you're back," Chris began. "Everything work out for Billie?"

Brenda shrugged. "Unfortunately, problems like hers can't be solved in one afternoon. The poor kid sat there in a corner cursing her parents, Tony, Garfield House, and me. Nothing I said seemed to make a difference. I feel so helpless."

Chris gave her a reassuring pat on the arm. "You showed her you care. That's got to mean something."

Brenda managed a smile. "I hope so."

"I suppose you're not in the mood then, to help me with a problem," Chris said, looking at her expectantly.

It had to be bad news. Brenda had seen a similar hurt expression on Billie's face all afternoon. Brenda stole a quick glance at her clock radio. She was already late for her date, but she couldn't bear to leave Chris when she so obviously needed someone to talk to. "Brad's picking me up in five minutes, but if you don't mind my running around the room while you talk, I'm all ears."

Chris sat down on the edge of Brenda's bed. "It's Ted," she said, picking nervously at her fingernails.

Brenda was searching through her jewelry box for the right pair of earrings. She shut her eyes momentarily against the returning memory of their dance at the party. The situation between Chris and Ted had deteriorated steadily since then.

"I wish I knew why. He won't let me watch him practice, and every time I ask about how it's going, he changes the subject — like it's none of my business."

"If Ted can't see what a good deal he's got with you, maybe you should cool it for a while."

"Oh, Brenda, you know I can't do that. Besides, he's like two different people these days. When we're with a group of kids, he's all lovey-dovey with me and jokes as usual, like a junior David Letterman. But whenever we're alone, it's like trying to talk to a stone wall."

"Now I know his problem. If he's staying up late enough to watch David Letterman, he's not getting enough sleep," Brenda said quickly. "Oh, I know that's not an answer, Chris. I just don't know what else to tell you."

"I'm afraid I'm losing him, Brenda," Chris said in a tiny voice.

Brenda turned around. Chris looked as if she were about to cry.

"Brenda, Brad's here," her mother called up the stairs. Brenda was torn. Chris needed her, but Brad didn't deserve to be stood up. "I could tell Brad another emergency came up," she said.

Chris waved her off. "No, don't worry. I'll be all right. Really, I will. Maybe a nice long shower will help. I've got a big day ahead of me tomorrow, with the interview in the afternoon and the banquet here at night."

Brenda hesitated.

"Go on and have a good time," Chris said, rising from the bed. Brenda grabbed her purse and headed for the door. She turned as she stood in the doorway.

"Don't worry, Chris. Everything's going to be okay. I'm sure of it."

Brad took Brenda to a miniature golf course near Bethesda. Brenda had passed by the brightly lit amusement area often, but she hadn't played the game since she was a little girl. She hoped it would take her mind off the problems that had now been heaped on her shoulders.

They picked up their balls and clubs from a building shaped like a little castle, passing by rows of deserted video and pinball games. Brenda chose a yellow ball for good luck. Not only was it her favorite color, but the ball also matched her shirt.

As Brenda teed up for the first hole, she noticed Brad writing on the scorecard with the stub of a pencil they gave him at the counter. "Don't tell me you're going to keep score," she cried out.

"It's no fun if we don't," he countered good-naturedly.

"Then I might as well throw in the towel right now. I never was very good at this." With that she smacked the ball right through the hole in the bottom of the windmill that straddled the green. It stopped about an inch from the cup, and she tapped it in.

"Beginners luck," she said, smiling apologetically.

Brad smiled knowingly. "A hustler, huh? Well, I'd better warn you. I'm the champion miniature golf player in the Davidson family." He set up his ball and methodically flicked his wrists a few times, testing his swing. He hit the ball squarely, and it fell into the cup.

"How about that, sports fans?" he cried.

"Uh, what did you say?" Brenda realized then that she'd momentarily spaced out.

"Hey, you missed my hole-in-one," Brad said.

"I'm sorry," Brenda replied. "My mind just doesn't seem to be on the game. I had a rough afternoon with Billie at Garfield House."

"Let's go on to the next hole," he said without giving her a chance to elaborate. "I'll go first this time."

Brenda made sure she caught all the action as Brad made another clean shot that landed about six feet away from the cup. Brenda's shot caromed the wrong way, and she ended up almost back where she'd started. It took her six swings to make the hole, compared to Brad's two.

"Hey, Brenda, did you hear about the change in plans for Duane's graduation party? So many people accepted his invitation that he's moving it to the country club. And I just heard Randy Nakamora's having a fiesta at his house, too."

"How many parties does that make — six?"

"Seven, I think. And we're going to all of them."

Brenda chatted almost automatically about graduation, but she was still thinking about Billie. Brenda had convinced the girl to stay the night at Garfield House, but she was afraid Billie might try to run away again — this time to another city. By the time they were halfway through the course, that alarming possibility was totally dominating her thoughts.

It was then she remembered that there was a pay phone outside the clubhouse. "I'll be right back," she told Brad as he set up for the tenth hole. "I've got a call to make."

"Can't it wait?" he asked.

"No, it's really important." She was already

headed back along the twisted concrete path.

Brenda found out that Billie was still at Garfield House, and she reassured the troubled girl that she'd come see her again after school the next day. Relieved, she headed back to Brad.

They had to wait while another couple played through the hole. "What was that all about?" he wondered.

"Billie. I had to make sure she's all right."

"You're going to see her tomorrow, aren't you? She'll be okay till then. Come on, let's have fun."

"But I am," she said. She gave Brad a kiss on the cheek and set her ball down for the next shot.

For the next three holes she listened while Brad told her about a prank some of the guys had pulled on his history teacher. Normally she would have thought it was as funny as he did, but tonight it sounded frivolous.

Brenda's mind shifted to Chris's problem. Her attempts to concentrate on golf were futile, and she finished the last hole far behind Brad, who carefully lined up at the last tee even though his victory was already assured. Brenda was growing impatient as he practiced his swing, then carefully lined up his hands on the putter. When the club thwacked the ball Brenda blurted out, "Has Ted told you anything lately?"

Brad was so startled he dropped the putter on his toe. He winced but didn't seem upset. "Ted? Except for some bad jokes, he hasn't told me anything noteworthy."

"Nothing about baseball . . . or about Chris?"

Brad was now leaning casually on his club. "Nothing," he repeated, looking her squarely in the eye. "Why all this sudden concern about Ted?"

"It's not him. It's Chris. Something's going on between those two."

"Probably another one of their periodic readjustments," he said. "All couples go through times like that."

Brenda felt as if Brad had just reached over and turned on a bright light above her head. Her own relationship with Brad deserved her attention, yet she had been taking it for granted, practically ignoring Brad. The Garfield House staff was taking good care of Billie. That's why they were there. And it was pointless to worry about Chris when there was nothing she could do for her anyway. Putting her arms around Brad's waist, she purred softly, "Let's not bother finishing up, okay? I'm handing you the championship on a silver platter."

The twinkle returned to Brad's brown eyes. "A Davidson always earns his trophies." He released himself from her grasp. "I've got to finish."

"Anything you say."

Because it was a school night and Brenda couldn't stay out late, Brad drove her home after a quick stop for sodas at Fritzbe's. He was still talking about the graduation parties, trying to figure out how to be in seven places at the same time. It was a dilemma he seemed to relish.

Brenda managed to keep up her end of the conversation, but in spite of her best efforts, she couldn't help thinking about Billie and all the other people staying at Garfield House. None of them would be celebrating graduation.

Chapter
13

As Brenda opened her locker the following afternoon she caught a glimpse of the quick blur of a boy in a familiar blue plaid shirt. She did a double take. It was Ted. Curious, she paused to watch as he reached the end of the crowded hall, then turned back.

"Slow down, Mr. Freight Train," Brenda called out as he reached her.

"Brenda," he said breathlessly, coming to a stop. "Have you seen Chris?"

"You just missed her."

Ted clenched his teeth. "She didn't even give me a chance to wish her good luck on her interview. I guess she doesn't think my support will make any difference in helping her get the job."

"She feels hurt, you know," Brenda told him.

"We both do."

Brenda slammed her locker shut. "You two should sit down and have a good talk together," she said, beginning to walk down the hall.

"It's hard to stop her long enough to talk these days." Ted sighed. "Brenda, can I be totally honest with you?"

"Of course."

"The longer Chris and I don't talk, the more I wonder if there's any point. Especially . . . especially when I can talk to someone like you, who really cares about what's happening to me."

"Ted," Brenda said, "I do care about you. And I'd like to talk, anytime you need it. But don't sell Chris short. She cares about you."

"I know that, Brenda. But lately it just doesn't seem to be enough."

Brenda could see that the pain in Ted's eyes was real, and she wanted to stay and comfort him. But at that moment, she knew, someone else was waiting for her. She reached for Ted's hand.

"Ted, I'd like to talk, but I've got to see someone who's expecting me at Garfield House."

Ted's eyes opened wide in new interest. "Really? Would it be okay if I came along?"

"It's not a fun place," she said, trying to discourage him. There was no way she could let him eavesdrop on her conversation with Billie.

"I know, but I'm real curious to see the place that's had such a big influence on you. In fact, I can drive you there. It'd be more comfortable than the bus."

Brenda was tempted by the offer. "I won't be able to spend much time with you. . . ."

111

"I don't mind hanging out in the hallway. You've talked so much about Garfield House, I want to see what it's like inside."

"Okay," she said reluctantly.

Brenda relaxed a little as she walked out to the parking lot with Ted. "I guess I do get a little carried away about that place. It's the real world, Ted — stuff you don't see much of around Rose Hill. I hope it doesn't bother you."

"I'm a big boy. I can take it," he said.

During the ride into the city Brenda filled Ted in about her work at Garfield House and her experience the day before with Billie. She got so caught up in what she was saying that she was still talking as Ted turned his car onto the Georgetown street where Garfield House was located. There was no time left now to ask him about Chris. "Well, here we are," she said.

From the outside Garfield House looked as tidy as the other colonial-style structures on the well-manicured street. Yet there was a sense that another world lay behind the steel-rimmed front door. Visible through a second story window was a young boy, staring out at them vacant-eyed.

"This place sure is lucky to have someone like you," Ted said.

"I was lucky to have it when I needed it."

As they walked up the neat but weather-worn painted concrete steps to the entrance, Ted added, "It takes a very special kind of person to do what you do."

Brenda thought the praise was a little extravagant, but then Ted didn't know places like this existed before he met her. Once inside, she introduced Ted to Tony Martinez, who agreed to show Ted around while Brenda was visiting Billie.

With some trepidation Brenda walked up the steps to Billie's third-floor room. She knocked, then slowly opened the door, mentally preparing herself for anything. She was surprised to see Billie lying on a freshly made bed, casually thumbing through a magazine. A blue canvas suitcase sat packed at the foot of the bed. Brenda gasped. "Billie?"

The younger girl raised her eyes, and Brenda noticed with delight she no longer had that look of a terrified, abandoned puppy she had when Brenda first met her. "Brenda!" she cried. Happily she jumped off the bed and threw her arms around a startled Brenda. "I'm going home," Billie announced. She was smiling behind the masses of dark hair that obscured her pretty face.

The two girls sat on the bed and talked. "My mom agreed to go for counseling if I would come home," Billie said.

"Billie, I am so happy to hear that," Brenda told her. "Just remember, there will probably still be some rough times. You know where to find me if you need me."

"You saved my life, Brenda," Billie said.

"Hey, no dramatics," Brenda answered. "All I did was hang out with you for a while — "

" — when nobody else would," Billie finished. "I'm never going to forget that."

Brenda felt elated. Billie still had a long way

to go before things would calm down for her at home, but now at least she was on the right road. Brenda left the room confident that she had been doing the right thing these past few days.

She spent more time than usual with Billie. Although she knew Billie's departure was a happy occasion, it was always hard to say good-bye to someone she had begun to care about. After giving Billie one last hug for luck, Brenda went to the front lobby to meet Ted and was surprised to find he wasn't there. A quick search found him shooting baskets with a couple of guys in the gym. He waved to her, took one last shot, and said good-bye to the other three boys on the court.

"Do you have to be home right away?" Ted asked as they walked toward the car.

"No," Brenda said, hesitating.

"Let's go to The American Cafe. I want to buy you dinner. This has been a great afternoon."

Brenda examined Ted's face over the top of the car. He looked like a different person from the sad, sullen guy she had seen in the hallway that afternoon. A good day was becoming a great day.

"I'd love to go to The American Cafe," Brenda said, welcoming the delay. It would be a nice buffer between Garfield House and the date she had planned with Brad later that evening.

Ted was unusually quiet as they waited for their food to be served. Brenda wasn't too surprised. Garfield House had that effect on lots of first time visitors. "It's quite a scene in there, isn't it?"

"Garfield House? Yes," he said. "Until now, my idea of big trouble was splashing paint on the Leesburg statue or TP-ing the principal's car. I spoke to a guy today who tried to set his own house on fire! Another guy just got out of a juvenile detention center and found out his parents had changed the locks on the house."

"Kind of trivializes our own problems, doesn't it?" Brenda commented.

"Yeah." Ted sighed deeply. "Unfortunately, it doesn't make them any less real."

It was the opening Brenda was waiting for. "Care to talk about it?"

Ted nodded. "Can you keep a secret?"

"Sure."

"Okay. The real reason I came with you was to get out of baseball practice today."

"Why?"

The waiter came by with their dinners: chicken crepes for Brenda and fettuccine for Ted. He picked up his fork and twirled the strands in an endless circle as he spoke. "The last two weeks have been like a bad dream for me. The humiliation of playing badly in front of my friends, the even bigger letdown of being chosen for a third-rate team. I could have dealt with that, as long as I knew I'd be playing with the top team soon. But after practicing all this week I don't see how I'm going to do it. The truth is I'm just not a good player. Even with the guys who play lousy

I'm making more than my share of mistakes. This never happened to me before."

Brenda took a deep breath. Ted wasn't going to like what she had to say. "Look, Ted, you're lucky to be very good at one thing — football. Those guys you just met . . . they'd give their eye teeth to have one-tenth the recognition and appreciation you've got. It's just hard for me to understand what you're talking about. So what if you're not a superstar baseball player?"

Ted whistled. "Boy, you really lay it on the line."

"It's called putting things in perspective."

Ted stared down at the sidewalk, watching the feet of the thickening crowd of Washingtonians hurrying home to start their weekends. "I wish the answer was that simple. Problem is, I'm not sure what the *question* is. See, what's bugging me goes beyond baseball. I've always thought that whatever I wanted to do, I'd be great at it whether it's sports or, down the line, whatever I end up doing for a living. Failing at baseball's made me realize I could fall flat on my face the next time I go after something I want."

"Or you could be great at it," Brenda countered. "Ted, it's easy to fall into the trap of thinking *everything* is terrible and nothing is ever going to work out right again. Believe me, I've been there. It's a bad head trip, but that's all it is." Brenda let out a nervous giggle. "I sound like something out of Psych. 101, don't I?"

There was a long pause before Ted answered.

"Funny, I guess I've always had a lot of expectations put on me — from my family, from Chris. As long as I delivered I never thought much about it. But now that I'm not, it's making me look at everything in a whole new light. I'm not sure what I want — and part of me is too scared to find out."

"Does Chris know this?" Brenda asked.

"No. Some of this is stuff I'm just starting to realize myself talking here with you."

"I think you ought to tell her."

"I'll try. But lately it's been hard to talk to her. She's got a lot on her mind, and I've always had trouble talking about my problems."

"You're not having trouble talking with me."

"It's different somehow," he said. "I feel very comfortable with you. And you've given me a lot to think about." His eyes looked deeply into hers.

Brenda happened to notice her watch as she picked at the remains of her meal. "Omigosh, we've got to hurry," she told Ted. "Brad's picking me up for the Madonna concert in two hours."

Ted lurched against the back of the bentwood chair. "Chris's got that honor society banquet tonight. I forgot all about it. I was sort of hoping the four of us could go out."

Brenda was too concerned about getting back in time to read much significance into the request. "Some other time, maybe."

"Yeah, I'd like that," Ted said. "I'd like that a lot."

Chapter 14

Chris was dressed and finishing a grapefruit half when Brenda made her way groggily into the kitchen. "How can you be so wide awake on a Saturday morning?" Brenda said, yawning as she groped for the refrigerator door. "It's positively inhuman."

Chris chuckled. "I'm not. It's the effect of these running clothes. You've never heard of a sleepy athlete, right?"

"I suppose," Brenda said, pouring herself a glass of milk.

"How was the concert?"

"Good . . . but loud," Brenda answered happily. The earsplitting music and festive crowd had made all attempts at conversation with Brad impossible. "And your banquet?"

Chris fiddled with her spoon. "Dad didn't have

anything to complain about. Everybody was gone by eleven."

"Including Ted?"

She nodded. "I really didn't expect him to stay long. He made an appearance, then left to play cards with Peter and some other guys."

Brenda leaned against the counter, facing Chris. "So you and he didn't talk?"

"Well, we talked but didn't *talk*. Why?"

"Oh, nothing," Brenda said, taking a big gulp of her milk. "Oh, I almost forgot; how'd your interview go?"

"I still don't know! I met the head of the office and he was nice and all, but our meeting only lasted five minutes. He asked me a few dumb questions about my family and school activities and that was it. The only thing he told me was that I'm one of three people still in the running — and Geraldine's not one of them! He said someone from the office would be getting back to me in the next several days."

"That's good news, isn't it?"

"Only if the wait doesn't kill me first." She got up, dumped her grapefruit rind in the garbage, and put her empty bowl in the dishwasher. "That's why I'm looking forward to my workout with Ted this morning. The running ought to help me unwind. That reminds me, Ted should have been here by now."

"Maybe he overslept," Brenda said.

"Hmm," Chris said. "I'd better give him a call."

She walked over to the wall phone and started dialing. Brenda drifted to the edge of the counter, pretending to read the newspaper her stepfather had dropped there before leaving for his weekly tennis game. She was expecting to overhear a major battle.

But there were no fireworks. There wasn't even a crackle. Chris was on the phone less than a minute, her back to Brenda. She turned around as soon as she finished the call. "Looks like Ted can't make it," she said sheepishly.

"What's wrong?"

"He woke up this morning with a frog in his throat. He think's he's coming down with a cold," Chris said, as she walked toward the back door.

"You going over to see him now?"

"No. He said he hardly ever gets sick, but when he does he likes to sleep for hours. He's hoping to shake this thing before baseball practice this afternoon."

"He told you that?"

"Yeah, but I wouldn't be surprised if he bailed out today. He sounded pretty bad." She zipped up the front of her running suit. "I still need to get this nervous energy out of my system. I'm going out for a run."

Brenda wanted to go after Chris and tell her all about the talk she and Ted had had in Georgetown. As a stepsister she somehow felt it was her duty. But she had promised Ted their conversation was secret. It was also possible that Ted really was telling the truth. If he'd truly listened

120

to her, he might have decided to hang in with the baseball team a while longer. If he did, then he would really want to make it to practice despite his cold.

At least that's what she hoped.

Sasha Jenkins stopped in at the sub shop to grab a snack before heading home. She'd just put in a hectic few hours at her parents' bookstore while they were out hunting for a new living room sofa. She settled into a booth with an Isaac Bashevis Singer anthology she'd brought from the store while she waited for her egg salad to arrive.

Soon she became aware of the conversation going on in the booth next to hers. Normally she wasn't one to eavesdrop, but she got more and more curious as she recognized one of the boys' voices as Ted's. Chris had told her that morning that he was home with a cold, but he sounded fine. She couldn't stop herself from listening.

"You'd have to pay me to set foot on that baseball field again," Ted said. "I'm big enough to admit when I've made a mistake, and I sure did with that sport." He snorted. "I shouldn't really call it a sport — it's a pastime for wimps." He and the boy with him started to laugh.

Sasha pressed herself against the wood-backed booth. This was too interesting to ignore, she rationalized, considering that her role as a school newspaper reporter entitled her to listen. Ted Mason was big news around campus, after all.

The other boy said, "I could have told you that in the first place and saved you the trouble . . . though I've got to admit I had a good laugh when I heard you didn't make the Yankees."

"Thanks, pal," Ted said grumpily. "That's all I need, guys on the football team deserting me. What's going to happen this fall? Is anyone going to want to go out on the field with me?"

"Sure, Ted. Look, I didn't know you were so touchy about this. I was just kidding around. Of course all the guys on the team are behind you."

"Yeah, I was just kidding, too," Ted said, though he said it too uneasily for Sasha to believe him. "We gridiron types always stand together, right, Mark?"

"You bet. It's the only game in town. Macho, man."

"That's what I didn't like about baseball," Ted went on. "It was wimps-ville. Standing around, waiting for some other guy to get going. What fun is that, I ask you? In football, you keep going all the time — whatever position you play. I mean, like, you need endurance and strength to make it through a game. That's why geeks like those guys I practiced with could never make it through even one period of football."

"So what does Chris say about this?"

"It doesn't matter," Ted said. "It's my decision."

Sasha's egg salad arrived, but she could barely eat it. The boy's voice was definitely Ted's but the arrogance made him sound like a stranger.

His last remark about Chris was the worst. She'd never known him to be disrespectful toward her.

Either Ted was talking big to impress his friend or he'd undergone a total personality change, Sasha concluded. In any event, it was bad news that would only be compounded if Ted discovered she'd overheard the whole conversation.

Her salad barely touched, she slipped out of the booth and headed for the front cash register.

As soon as she got home she tried to get Chris on the phone, but there was no answer. After giving it some thought, though, she was glad she couldn't reach Chris. Sasha believed that, as a reporter, it was unconscionable to publish a story without all the facts. Following that logic, it would be practically immoral for a friend like her to repeat snatches of conversation she'd heard out of context. She might hurt Chris needlessly — and she'd rather spend the rest of her life dining on junk food than do anything to harm her friend.

Chapter
15

"Shawn, I'm going to kill you!"

Chris laughed at Phoebe's fuming. Her younger brother, Shawn, had just poured a plastic pailful of water over her head, flattening her red hair around her face like a copper helmet. Little, wet dark lines were forming on her turquoise-and-yellow striped bathing suit.

"Hey, what are you complaining about? You're sitting in the water," Shawn asked as he scampered to the deep end of his aunt's swimming pool. It was rectangular with a small Jacuzzi at one end. Phoebe was sitting inside the Jacuzzi along with Chris and Sasha, whom she'd invited to cool off with her on this sticky Sunday afternoon. Her aunt was away for the weekend and had given them permission to be there. Phoebe wished her aunt had left her brother off the invitation list.

"Warm water," she hissed back at him. "That pool water is *cold*." She slunk back down into the whirling water until it reached her ears. She mumbled, "One of these days I'm going to find a country where murdering a brother isn't a capital offense."

"Try Antarctica," Sasha suggested.

"There's no country there," Phoebe said.

"Where there's no country, there are no laws," Sasha reasoned.

Phoebe shook her head. "Too cold — even for fratricide," she said. Then she turned the jets and bubbles on full blast, making further conversation impossible for the moment.

Chris watched as Shawn did a bellyflop off the diving board. Suddenly the cooler pool looked inviting. After a minute or so of being blasted by the full jets, she pulled herself up onto the Jacuzzi's blue tiled rim, letting her long legs dangle in the water. Sasha followed a moment later, leaving only Phoebe resting peacefully in the warm water, her eyes closed, looking as if she had ventured some place at least as far away as Antarctica. Chris wished her mind were at rest and she could feel so peaceful. As it was she felt like a jigsaw puzzle box with pieces from several puzzles thrown into it — nothing fit right.

Sasha turned off the Jacuzzi. "Shawn!" Phoebe cried, opening up her eyes.

"Don't blame him. It was me," Sasha said,

twisting her long brown hair into a makeshift braid. "I'm dying to know what you were dreaming about. Was it Michael?"

"No," Phoebe said, playfully splashing water in Sasha's direction. "I don't know how many times I've got to pound it into your head that we're just friends. If you really want to know, I was thinking about a new song I heard over the radio yesterday. I can't get it out of my mind."

"Is that the name of it?" Chris asked.

"No. I don't know what it's called . . . or who does it, either. Do you? Listen." Phoebe started humming a bouncy song Chris couldn't identify.

"You could call up Monica or Peter. I'll bet they'll know."

"It's not that important," Phoebe said. "By the way, is Ted feeling better today?"

"He sounded better when I called him this morning. Do you realize last night was the first Saturday in ages I haven't been out with him? I found out *The Love Boat* was still on TV."

"I could have told you that," Phoebe said.

"But I could have just as easily watched it at his house," Chris grumbled. "I don't know why he made himself off-limits to me all day yesterday. It's not like a cold's some dread disease."

"I can't remember the last time Ted was sick. Maybe he's got this weird thing about germs," Phoebe wondered.

Chris looked at Sasha, who was looking at her

as if she were speaking a foreign language. "What do you think, Sash?"

"You say Ted stayed inside all day yesterday?"

"Why are you looking at me like that?" Chris asked.

"Uh, the sun's in my eyes," Sasha said. She added hesitantly, "Maybe Ted's caught in a low biorhythm."

"Something about him's definitely off," Chris said. "I feel like he's hiding something from me."

"Why don't you go to his house and confront him?" Sasha asked. "It's the easiest way to find out."

"No, it isn't," Chris said. "For the past week or so every time I've asked him a direct question he clams up. If I go to his house he'll get mad at me for invading his privacy or something weird like that."

"Do you think he might be jealous of your summer job?" Phoebe wondered.

"That's ridiculous," Chris said. "For one thing, I don't have it yet. For another, it's not something he'd ever want to do. For yet another, he'll be busy playing baseball this summer."

"But maybe it's not as farfetched as you think. You may not have the job yet, but it's all you've been talking about. And coming at the same time as his baseball experience it may be making him feel uneasy."

Chris thought about that. "He *has* been sensitive about baseball all week long. But I've told him where he plays or how he does makes no difference to me."

"But it could make a difference to him," Phoebe said pointedly.

"I won't know for sure till I talk to him. Maybe I'll find a good excuse to just happen to go by his practice later this afternoon. I've been wanting to see how he's been doing anyway." Chris stood up. "I need to clear my mind. I'm going to do a few laps. Anyone want to join me?"

"No," Phoebe and Sasha spoke out in unison.

"Sissies." She scrunched her nose as she marched to the pool's edge.

Sasha moved closer to Phoebe. "I've got a problem. If you knew that a friend's boyfriend was lying to her, would you tell her?"

Phoebe shot back in a whisper, "Ted's lying to Chris?"

"He's not home, deadly ill. He was at the sub shop yesterday. I heard him saying he quit the baseball team and that he didn't care how Chris felt about it."

"What a jerk!" Phoebe cried.

Chris's head rose above the water, as if she'd overheard. But just as quickly she ducked underwater again and continued her graceful strokes.

"Ssh!" Sasha warned. "So should I tell her?"

Phoebe thought about it. "If you tell her now, she'll wonder why you've kept it from her for a day. If I were you, I'd keep my mouth shut. She's going to find out soon enough when she goes down to the ball field."

Sasha glanced back at her friend, now gliding slowly toward the far end of the pool. The swim seemed to relax her, Sasha noted with relief. Yet the more Sasha watched, the more she felt she was looking into the eye of a hurricane. Chris may have appeared cool and calm, but just beyond the horizon a terrible storm was brewing.

Chapter
16

Chris decided to walk to Briarwood Park. The rampant electricity inside her was still there despite her swim, and she figured the three-mile trek would help calm her down. She'd always enjoyed the sight of the late-spring blooms along Briarwood Road, the street on which the field was located. A slight breeze had arisen, too, making the trip a pleasurable way to cool off.

But Chris was still worried about Ted. She still wasn't sure what she was going to say to him. She wasn't even convinced he'd be happy to see her or if he'd be mad at her having come. He might not even want to talk to her, she realized, amazed at the thought that their relationship could have come to this.

When she neared the field, she saw a sea of red-and-white uniforms. RAMBLERS was written across the bright red shirts in white script letters.

All the boys were wearing white baseball caps, which made it hard for Chris to pick out Ted. She felt another pang of hurt when she realized Ted hadn't told her his number.

As she walked toward home plate someone waved at her with a fielder's glove. "Hi, Chris!" the boy shouted.

Expectantly Chris looked at the bench. Then she sighed. The boy waving to her was Walt Weston. "Hi," she answered as she approached him. "Have you seen Ted?"

Walt shook his head. "He hasn't been around here since Thursday."

"Not since Thursday?" she asked. Walt nodded. "Do you know why?"

Walt shrugged. "Thursday's when they handed out the uniforms. Maybe he didn't like his."

"I don't think so," Chris managed to say. Walt shrugged again.

"Why don't you ask the coach?" Walt asked. He pointed to a tall, rugged, dark-haired man wearing rugby shorts talking to the first baseman.

Chris walked up to him. "Excuse me," she said. "My name's Chris Austin. I'm a friend of Ted Mason."

The man extended his hand and gave Chris a firm, strong handshake. "Dieter Heinz," he said, smiling. "What can I do for you?"

"I understand Ted hasn't been here since Thursday. Do you know why?"

The man snorted. "I wish I knew. I guess he lost interest. A lot of guys do."

"Yeah," Chris said, her voice trailing. She

131

didn't know what else she could say. "Uh, thanks for your help."

"If you see Ted, tell him I'd like him to come back. He was starting to show some promise."

"I will."

Chris walked away in a daze, somehow managing to find herself headed in the right direction. Now, more than ever, she was determined to find Ted. Why hadn't he shown up at practice these past few days? Even more important, why hadn't he told her? The cold would explain Saturday's absence, but not Friday's.

Ted obviously had quit the team. Chris thought back to their brief talks during the week. She'd known he wasn't totally happy with the way things were going, but he'd never given her any indication it had come to this.

She turned up the street that led to Ted's house, full of hurt, anger, and worry. How could he have lied to her? Why couldn't he confide in her? When she reached Ted's house, she only learned that the MG wasn't out front, and nobody was home to answer the door. With nowhere else to go, she headed home.

Her stepmother was outside, weeding the patch of ivy on the steep front lawn. "Hi, Chris," she called. "How was your swim?"

It felt like years since she'd been in the pool. She slipped the knapsack with her wet suit inside off her back. "Fine," she said dispiritedly.

"Oh, I almost forgot. Ted was here a while ago."

Chris blinked her eyes in disbelief. "He was? When?"

"Oh, about an hour or so," Catherine answered, still kneeling in the ivy patch.

"Did he say where he was going?"

"I didn't speak with him. All I know is that he took Brenda with him."

Chris sat down on the front step to think. Another mismatched piece had been added to the puzzle. She'd told Ted she was spending the afternoon with Phoebe, and yet he had come to the house anyway.

Shaking her head, she went inside and up to her room. All that walking had tired her out. Chris fell on her bed and into a dreamless sleep.

The only thing running through Brenda's mind was: What am I doing here?

Ted had driven her to a diner in Chevy Chase. As he handed her the menu he said, "Go on, order anything you want. It's on me."

Brenda took it, still feeling as if she were dream-walking through a very odd experience. With Brad busy entertaining visiting relatives, she'd decided to devote the afternoon to such mundane activities as washing her socks, cleaning out her closet, and ironing the shirts that had lain in a wrinkled heap there for months.

She'd just finished running the iron over a particular favorite of hers, a bright green cotton button-down with electric-blue and pink flowers, when Ted showed up in the laundry room. He'd told her to unplug the iron and come with him. He wouldn't tell her where or why, but his energy, which seemed to have returned completely after so many days of moping, was irresistible. Brenda had been sure Ted's mysterious manner meant he wanted her help on some secret surprise for Chris.

Quickly she glanced at the menu. It offered nothing but hamburgers prepared in forty different ways. "I'll have a 27," she said. She wasn't sure what was on it. She just liked the number.

After the waitress took their order, Ted asked, "Like this place? I found it yesterday."

That remark only added to Brenda's confusion. "I thought you were at home sick."

Ted smiled slyly. "You really didn't believe that, did you?"

"No," she said sheepishly. "Why'd you make it up?"

Ted looked directly at Brenda. She found his stare discomforting. "I thought a lot about what you said the other night, about not being afraid to try new things," he told her. "Well, that's what I did yesterday — and it was great. I got in my car and spent most of the morning driving all over the county. I never realized there were so many neat places I'd never seen before. Like the waterfall outside Glenn Hills, some neat trails along the C & O canal. There's a guy on a farm near Norbeck who's got a great collection of antique cars."

Brenda thought quickly. Ted had to have

logged well over a hundred miles. "That was some trip you took."

"It wasn't just a physical one. I had to sort out my mind, Brenda. So many things have happened so quickly . . . you know what I mean?"

"Not really," she said. "You still haven't explained why you lied to Chris."

Ted took a sip of water. "You know, I never knew you had that scar over your eye."

"That?" Reflexively Brenda smoothed her index finger over her right eyebrow. It hid a tiny scar she'd gotten from knocking into a table when she was a baby. She hardly thought about it anymore. It was so barely noticeable no one could tell it was there unless they stared at her. With a start she realized Ted had not taken his eyes from her since they'd sat down. "It's nothing," she said, easing her chair slightly away from the table.

"It's part of you, so that makes it something," he said. "There's so much about you I hardly know."

"I don't have too many secrets," Brenda said, feeling more uncomfortable with each passing second. She wished she'd never left home.

Still concentrating his attention on her, Ted poured ketchup on his burger, which had just arrived. "That conversation we had the other day really opened my eyes. I was getting myself into a negative think trap, I think that's what you called it. Once I realized what it was I started asking myself why. And I came up with this answer: I'd got myself into a real rut. Always going to the same places, seeing the same people, doing the same things. I need a change, Brenda, and if we hadn't had that talk I might never have seen that."

Brenda silently pushed the french fries on her plate around with her fork.

Ted took a large bite of his burger. "These are great, aren't they — hey, you're not eating!"

"I'm not hungry," she said nervously. Why had he brought her here?

"Brenda, I know this is kind of sudden, but something happened to me after that trip to Garfield House. I haven't been able to stop thinking about you."

"You — you don't really mean that."

"Yes, I do."

"Ted, you know how I feel about Brad."

"Do I? From what I've seen and heard, you two seem to be on different wavelengths, at least as much as Chris and I are, and — "

"And nothing." Brenda shook her head. "I don't know what you saw or heard, but things with Brad and me are fine."

"Really?" He raised an eyebrow.

"What's that supposed to mean?"

"You practically ignored him at the party, and at lunch the other day you turned away when he started talking about how he can't wait to see the yearbook."

"Do you know how many times I've heard him say that?" she asked.

"Then there's been all the talks we've had — at the sub shop, in D.C."

Brenda shook her head. "You had a problem. I wanted to help you out," she explained.

"Are you sure there isn't more to it than that?" Ted asked hopefully.

Brenda paused. Ted was making a dreadful mistake, and considering his fragile ego she wanted to let him down gently. "I think of you as my friend, Ted. You're a nice guy and — and — very easy to get along with. But that's as far as it goes. And even if there were more, I could never hurt Chris."

Ted leaned forward and grabbed Brenda's hands. "What if Chris weren't your sister?"

Brenda pulled away from his grasp and sighed heavily. "Ted, Chris *is* my sister. That's the only reason I'm here."

"But — " Ted looked up at her, with hurt in his eyes.

"There are no buts," she said. "Ted, I really would like to leave now." She rose and walked toward the door, not waiting to see if Ted was behind her. She waited for him beside the car.

As they left the parking lot, Brenda was almost afraid to speak. "Please drop me off at Brad's," she asked.

"Sure," Ted said dully. He started up the engine.

"Go talk with Chris," she added, speaking softly. "She needs you."

"I'm not so sure about that," he said. "She's such a perfectionist and so ambitious and all — I don't think I can keep up with her anymore."

Brenda turned from the window to face him.

"What is it with you two? Are you in a road race or a relationship?"

Ted jammed the clutch into gear. "We've been on different planets lately," he said, peeling out of the parking lot, tires screeching. "She's so excited about this high-powered job of hers, while I'm flopping around as a grunt on the baseball diamond. Did I tell you the real reason I quit? The coach didn't make me one of the starters. I couldn't even make it on the third-rate team."

"But I thought the whole point of summer baseball was to have fun."

"Fun? All it's done is drive Chris away from me."

"No," Brenda said sharply, moving forward in her seat. "*You*'ve put the distance between Chris and yourself. Chris has been tearing her hair out these past few days, worried sick about you. Did you know that?"

Ted looked surprised. "I thought she was obsessed with that job."

"Sure, it's important to her. But so are you, Ted. If you two break up now, she'll be devastated. Believe me."

"I'm not so sure."

"That's not surprising. Every time she's tried to get close to you recently, you've cut her off. You haven't given her a chance to show her concern."

Ted lowered his head, staring straight ahead at the road.

"I'm right, aren't I?" Brenda persisted.

"Yeah," he muttered.

"Do me a favor, please? Just talk to her. Give her a chance to straighten things out. Don't shut her out because you want to explore other things . . . explore them with her. She might like to see something different, too."

Ted fiddled with the rearview mirror before answering. Finally he said, "Okay."

Brenda smiled. "Ted," she began, "now can I ask you a question about a different subject?"

"Sure."

"Does it really seem as if I've been ignoring Brad?"

"Well," Ted said slowly, "maybe I have been looking for evidence. But it doesn't seem as though it's been too hard to find."

"Thanks, Ted. I think maybe you're right. But keep watching — I promise a big change."

Chapter
17

When Ted pulled up to Brad's house, Brenda leaned over and kissed him on the cheek. "I hope we can still be friends," she said.

"I think so," Ted said. His voice wasn't nearly as assured as the smile on his face. "And I promise I'll have that talk with Chris."

"Take care," she said. "I'll see you in school tomorrow."

Anxiously she rang the doorbell. Mrs. Davidson answered. "Why, Brenda, what a pleasant surprise," she said.

"Is Brad in?" Brenda asked. "I'd like to speak with him.

"He's in the kitchen. Won't you come in?"

Brenda found her own way through the quiet house. Brad was standing over the sink, loading dishes into the dishwasher and not looking too happy about it. "Hi, Brad," she said. "Surprise!"

Brad hesitated before facing her. "That gets my vote for the understatement of the year. What's up?"

Brenda slipped her index fingers through the belt loops of her khaki shorts. Brad didn't look too thrilled to see her. She clenched the loops tighter as a sense of panic flooded over her. This is going to be hard, she told herself. "I guess you could say I got an irresistible urge to see you," she said, trying to keep her voice calm and clear.

"I don't know how much fun you can have watching me load dishes," he said. He spun around the top rack, looking for an empty spot to put a coffee cup.

"Would you like some help?"

"No, I'm almost done." He continued to load a few more cups, hardly looking at her at all. "I'm the lucky guy who always gets to do cleanup whenever my aunt and uncle come over for Sunday dinner."

"Do you have to go back and entertain them?"

"No, they're already gone," he said flatly.

Brenda ventured a few steps closer and leaned her elbows on the counter. The small talk was only making her jumpier. "Brad, I've really got to talk with you. Right now."

Quickly he turned around. His tired eyes looked sad. "Yeah, I want to talk to you, too. But not here. Give me a minute to finish this up. Then we'll go out for a walk."

They were silent until Brad led her down the oak-lined sidewalk outside his house. It was dusk and the neighborhood was eerily quiet. Even the crickets were mute. Brenda had to start somewhere. "I was with Ted this afternoon." She looked at him as they walked, even though his eyes were directed at the view straight ahead. "He thinks I'm ignoring you."

"Aren't you?"

"Would I be here if I were?"

"Look, Brenda, there's a lot I've been meaning to say to you, too. We might as well be truthful and quit playing games with each other."

"I haven't been playing games with you."

"No? What do you call it when you can't see me two nights in a row — because of homework and a filling? Then when you see me, your mind is someplace else the whole time."

Brenda was distressed by the heaviness in his voice. He was a lot angrier at her than she ever had seen him.

Brad stopped walking. He took her hands in his. "I'm serious, Brenda. Two weeks ago I told you I wanted to make my last weeks in high school the best ever. I couldn't think of a better way of doing that than with you. But you've been giving me this flip-flop number. One day you're attentive and loving as ever, the next you're too busy to give me the time of day. That's not fair."

"Aren't you exaggerating just a little? I've been spending as much time with you as ever. Didn't we go out last night?"

"Last night you were more preoccupied with Chris and her problems than with me."

"She's going through a hard time," Brenda explained.

"Well, maybe I am, too." He ran his hand through his hair. "I've been thinking about this a lot, and I think I finally figured out what you're doing. But as I said, I don't like games, so let's make this a clean break."

Brenda felt as though she had been kicked in the stomach. "You can't mean that!" she cried.

"I thought I was speaking clearly enough. The way I see it, it's better if we cool things off now rather than let them drag on any longer. I want to at least have happy memories to hold on to, not a lot of fighting and disappointment." Brad was talking in his usual calm voice, which made the words take on an even eerier resonance.

Brenda stopped dead in her tracks, too numb to move. Where had she been when all this was brewing in Brad's head? "Is that really what you want?" she asked incredulously. The tension inside made her voice come out sounding squeaky and childish.

"It's what you want, isn't it?" Brad put his hands in the pockets of his dress pants.

"Are you speaking for me?"

"I don't have to. Your actions have been talking for you. When you backed off into a corner at my party I started thinking you must be losing interest in me. The feeling got stronger after you said you didn't want to see me."

"That's ridiculous," she said. "I deliberately stayed in the background at your party, yes, but

143

that was because I didn't want to hog center stage. As far as the other nights go, things came up that were out of my control. I wasn't trying to avoid you."

Brad kicked a pebble several feet along the concrete path. "I don't know. I'm going to be pretty busy working at the hospital this summer. With your job in D.C., I'm just not sure how much time we're going to be able to spend together. Then in the fall I'll be at Princeton. Who knows how many weekends I'll be able to come home? I hear the first semester's the roughest. If we can't make the effort to keep this thing together now, we'll never last then."

"Does that mean that you intend to break up with me anyway?" It seemed impossible to her he would do it so suddenly.

"I thought that's what you wanted."

"I never told you that."

"Maybe I can't imagine you sitting around waiting for me. It's better if I don't tie you down your senior year."

"Tie me down to what? I guess we've never talked about it, but I just took it for granted we'd find a way to continue even after you got to Princeton. You know, I'm not the kind of girl who slits her throat if she doesn't have a date every Saturday night. If I knew you still cared about me, I'd gladly stay home all year. I thought you knew that." She gave a ragged sigh.

Brad toed the pebble he had kicked ahead and gave it another shot. This time it rolled into the grass. "I did. But as far as I could tell, you'd changed your mind. . . ."

"Look, Brad — " Brenda's voice was shaky now, as she fought to hold back her tears. " — I'm sorry if I've spoiled your last days as a senior. I — I didn't mean to, believe me. But don't jump to the wrong conclusions . . . I mean, I'll try and make it up to you. . . ."

Brad stopped walking and turned toward Brenda. "You mean you still care about me?"

"I never stopped," she said, reaching gently for his arm.

Brad reached around her and pulled her tightly against him. "Brenda, I love you. But I'm not the totally confident guy everybody at Kennedy assumes I am. I need you . . . as much as Chris and the people at Garfield House do."

Brenda closed her eyes and held herself tightly against his familiar, solid warmth. Hadn't all her experience at Garfield House taught her to reach out to people, before they got desperate, not to take people for granted — especially the ones you cared about most? She pressed her face against his chest to stop a tear from sliding down her cheek.

"I love you, too," she whispered.

After they pulled back from their embrace they continued their walk about the neighborhood, arm in arm, enjoying the cooling breeze that had come with the setting sun. Brenda felt relieved now that they'd cleared the air, kissed, and made up. Still, there was one nagging thought

145

that she couldn't get rid of. "There's something else that's been bothering me lately," she told him. "It's minor in the grand scheme of things, but since we're being honest with each other I thought I'd bring it up."

"What is it?"

"Can we find something to talk about other than graduation?"

He gave her a lopsided smile. "I guess I've had a one-track mind about that. Sure, let's talk about how beautiful you look tonight. . . ."

He readily agreed to drive her home. As he pulled his car out of the driveway Brenda gazed at his handsome profile. She sighed wistfully, her mind rewinding back to the days when the thought of just talking to a guy like him — let alone dating him — seemed as remote a possibility as snow on the equator. Brad was too precious to let slip through her fingers.

His voice broke into her thoughts. "They say the yearbooks will finally be coming out tomorrow," he said excitedly.

Brenda felt a strange sensation in the pit of her stomach. The moratorium on graduation talk had lasted exactly ten minutes. "Oh, really?" she said lamely. "I bet you can't wait to see your pciture." She didn't know why she said that — she already knew the answer.

"Yeah," Brad answered, his eyes sparkling. "It's the day of reckoning. When everyone gets to find out what everybody really thinks of them," he said for perhaps the hundredth time in the past month. "Holly's so worried she might even stay home tomorrow."

"But she's one of the most popular seniors," Brenda said incredulously. "Everybody's going to want her to sign their books."

"That's the problem. She doesn't know what she's going to say."

"Still?" Brenda had been with her back in March when this topic had come up for the first time.

Brad continued, "I told her to write, love, Holly, over her picture, but somehow that's not good enough for her. She wants to write something that's going to make everyone remember her twenty years from now. In a way I can understand that."

I know. I was there when you told her that, Brenda wanted to scream. The knot in her stomach was now creeping up into her chest. But she forced herself not to make an issue of it. After all, she reasoned, in two weeks graduation would be over and so would all the ridiculous rituals associated with it. After that she and Brad could go back to discussing things that concerned just the two of them.

"I want you to be the first to sign my book," Brad said.

"I think I'll just write, love, Brenda. I don't like the idea of the whole school reading something personal," she said.

"If you insist, I'll hide it," he said, chuckling. He didn't take the note of concern in her voice that seriously. "I want you to be sincere. Twenty years from now when I dust off the old book, I'd like to look back fondly at my old high school sweetie."

Brenda now felt her throat constrict. Brad had tossed off that remark so casually — as if he'd already pigeon-holed her in the box of his life marked *high school*. Would he have another girl in the box marked *Princeton* . . . and another in the one marked *medical school?*

Don't make an issue of it, she told herself sternly. She turned to him, forcing a smile. She'd already cleared the air about their relationship once that evening and realized there was nothing to be gained by getting upset over what had to have been a careless remark. As long as everything was going her way — as it seemed to be right then — she told herself she had nothing to worry about.

Chapter
18

Her vivid nightmare was still too real to
shake when Chris woke up, and it came back as
vividly as ever when she walked into the kitchen
and saw Brenda sitting at the table eating a bowl
of cereal. Her stepsister looked happy and totally
at peace with herself. Why shouldn't she? Chris
thought to herself. She had the two most desirable
boys at Kennedy High throwing themselves at
her feet.

Chris backed into the living room before
Brenda spotted her. It was just as well, she reasoned; she didn't feel like eating anyway, even
though there was a giant emptiness in her stomach.

Now that she'd had time to think about everything, the pieces of the puzzle were finally starting to fall into place. Ted's uneasiness with her,

his lying about the baseball team and about his being sick were symptoms of what was really wrong with him: He had lost interest in her. It was as simple as that. She hadn't wanted to believe it, but now the evidence was too overwhelming to ignore. And finding out that he and Brenda had gone off together had clinched it. Now Chris realized what had happened: Brenda and Ted had fallen for each other.

Chris was too angry at Brenda to confront her, and too upset and hurt to talk about it with anyone else. She went through her Monday morning classes like a zombie, unable to pay attention to any of the work. For the first time in ages she didn't contribute to any of her class discussions. She might not have bothered coming to school for all the good it was doing her.

During lunch she hid out in the library, burying herself inside one of the carrels next to the English literature section. She told herself she'd retreated there to finish a homework assignment she hadn't completed because she'd fallen asleep early the night before. It was only partly true. Ordinarily she'd have tackled the work out on the quad, surrounded by the newsy chatter of her friends. But she still wasn't in the mood to socialize. She was also afraid that if she went out there she'd have to endure the painful sight of Brenda and Ted sitting together.

Somehow she managed to get through the day. Right after the last bell she ran out of Kennedy. She retreated to the sanctuary of her room, to nurse her misery and figure out how she was going to deal with the whole mess. Sooner or later, she realized, she'd have to face the two of them again, but at the moment, *later* sounded a whole lot better than sooner.

Eventually, she was unable to avoid the problem any longer, living in the same house with one of the people she was hiding from. It was then that Brenda threw open her bedroom door and burst into her room. "So there you are!" Brenda cried. "I've been looking all over for you!"

Chris wished she'd remembered to lock the door. "I don't feel like talking," she said as she turned her head toward the window. After a day of threatening clouds overhead it had finally begun to rain. Little droplets were running down the panes, obscuring the view.

Brenda sounded puzzled. "What's wrong, Chris? Are you mad at me?"

"Don't I have a right to be?" Chris rasped, turning to face her stepsister. "Or are you that insensitive?" It was then she noticed Brenda's dark matted hair. She'd obviously been caught in the storm. For a moment Chris's resolve to remain aloof weakened. Then she thought of Ted and Brenda together, laughing and talking, and her fury returned.

Shaking her wet head, Brenda came inside and closed Chris's door. She pulled out her desk chair and sat down. "This doesn't make sense. I thought I was doing the right thing."

"How could you?" Chris cried, sitting up.

"You know how I feel about Ted."

"I know — that's why I did what I did."

Chris folded her arms against her chest. "What are you talking about?"

"Would you rather I hadn't got involved?"

Chris stared at Brenda long and hard. She thought it was a funny question to ask. On the other hand, the concern she saw in Brenda's face was equally puzzling. "I don't know," she said, sighing. "I suppose if it hadn't been you it would have been someone else."

"I'm not so sure," Brenda said. "I think the reason Ted sought me out was because I'm your stepsister."

"But how could you go along with it?" Chris wanted to know. "I — I feel so betrayed."

"I'm sorry you feel that way. I didn't mean to tell Ted anything you didn't want him to know. I was only doing what I could to help you two stay together."

Chris didn't say anything for a long time. Then slowly it dawned on her that she and Brenda were having two completely different conversations. "You mean all you did was *talk* yesterday?"

"Sure. What did you think . . . Chris, don't tell me you thought Ted and I — " Shaking her head vigorously, she left the sentence unfinished.

But Chris completed it. " — were sneaking around behind my back? Yes," she admitted. "That's the way it looked to me. I was so mad at you I didn't even want to know anything about it.

Then I had this dream last night. . . . You know how hard it can be to shake a bad dream?"

"Oh, Chris, how could you ever think I'd do something like that! The only reason I left the house with Ted was to try to talk some sense into him. Didn't he tell you?"

"I haven't seen him all day."

Brenda hopped off the chair. "You mean he hasn't spoken to you at all?"

"No."

"But he promised!"

Chris leaned forward and motioned Brenda to join her on the bed. "Please tell me what happened yesterday. All I know is that you left the house with him and that he knew I wasn't going to be around."

Brenda pursed her lips. "This is really something you and Ted should discuss," she said.

"Please tell me, Brenda. Ted's been shutting himself off from me for days. I've got to know."

Brenda paused and gave a deep sigh. " I promised him I wouldn't tell you this. But since he broke his promise to me and hasn't talked to you, I guess I can break mine, too. I know he cares about you, Chris, but he's very confused right now. He thinks you're too preoccupied with your own life to care about him."

"That's ridiculous," Chris said.

"I know. That's what I told him, too. I think I finally got through to him, but since he hasn't talked to you it's kind of hard to tell."

"Well, that may not be his fault. I've kind of been hiding out all day."

"Tell me about it," Brenda said. "I went to all the usual hangouts after school till I finally got the bright idea that you might be here. For all we know, Ted could be looking for you right now."

"But what do you think he'll do?"

"Honestly, I don't know. To tell you the truth, after I left him last night I didn't have much time to dwell on our conversation. You're not the only one who's going through a crisis in her relationship."

"Don't tell me you and Brad — "

She nodded. "We almost broke up last night. Yesterday was some day for me — going from Ted to him. But I think things have sorted themselves out."

"Where was I when all this was going on? Don't tell me I've been tuning you out, too?"

"Uh uh. I just found out about it last night myself. I was the one who was tuning out Brad." She laughed. "You should have seen me making up for it at lunch today. I was all over him, cutting up his sandwich, stacking stuff on his tray . . . Sasha wondered if I was practicing for a home ec final."

"You have to admit it doesn't sound much like you."

"Well, I may have gone a little overboard, but I wanted to drum it into his thick skull that I care about him."

Brenda was interrupted by the sound of the phone. Chris picked it up on the first ring. "Hello?"

A few minutes later she put down the receiver. "That was Ted," she told Brenda, her voice full of apprehension. "He's on his way over."

Chapter
19

As Chris waited for Ted she wondered if he had remembered to fix that hole in his convertible top. She wiped a tear from her eye. Never in her wildest imaginings had it occurred to her that thinking about the top of a convertible would make her cry, how dumb. Then it dawned on her that she may have already taken her last ride in that car — and she would never know whether or not the hole was still there.

But when Ted finally knocked, Chris forgot about the punctured roof. As she opened the door, she felt suddenly shy. It took all her courage to look at him as she said hello.

The feeling seemed to be mutual. Ted slipped off his wet Kennedy High windbreaker and hung it on the oak coat rack next to the door. "Hi," he echoed. "Sure is wet out there."

"Let's go out to the kitchen. I'll make you some hot chocolate."

"I'd like that." He followed her into the kitchen and sat down at the table. Rapping his fingers on the wooden top, he asked nervously, "Did Brenda tell you anything?"

"Not really," she replied evasively.

"I was going to call you last night. I mean — I have so much to say to you. But when I picked up the phone I got scared and hung up." He chuckled nervously. "Can you imagine that, me being scared to talk to you?"

"You've been acting like you were scared to talk to me all week long."

"So Brenda *did* say something."

"I figured that one out by myself."

Quickly he responded, "How? I sure don't know which way I'm going these days. I used to think I knew myself pretty well, but now everything seems so complicated."

"Welcome to the club," Chris said.

"What do you mean? You always know exactly what you're doing."

Chris shook her head. "Maybe I look like I do, but I think anyone our age who says they're totally together is either lying or boring." She turned the flame on under the kettle and sat down next to him. "I've got a secret to tell you. I'm one of the most insecure people I know. I'm surprised you haven't figured that out after all the time we've spent together."

Ted just shrugged. Chris found it too difficult

to look at him, so she got up and walked over to the kitchen sink. Staring out the window over the sink, she noticed it had stopped raining, and the sun was making a valiant attempt to cut through the clouds. "I guess I've become good at hiding it," she continued. "But I don't always know if I'm doing the right things for the right reasons or going about stuff in the right way. In fact I think it's insecurity that sort of drives me to get A's in school and makes me try to get elected to student offices, and things. I keep pushing to succeed, I think, because I'm afraid if I stop I'm going to find out there's nothing there — that deep down I'm a big zero." Stopping abruptly, she spun around on her heel. "Do you ever feel that way about yourself?"

Ted seemed reluctant to look her in the eye. "I never stopped to think about stuff like that before. I mean, there I was: Ted Mason, the guy who plays football, tells jokes, wins cheeseburger-eating contests . . . it all seemed to come so easily. So when I decided to play baseball I figured that would be a piece of cake, too. But it didn't quite work out that way — and for the first time in my life I'm failing at something I really wanted to do. It's made me question everything else about my life, made me wonder if maybe I'll be a failure at other things I try to do."

"And the way I constantly talked about my big, prestigious summer job only made things worse, right?" Chris asked. Remembering

Phoebe's comment, she added nervously, "You must have felt like I was practically throwing it in your face."

"Well. . . ."

"It's okay — if you felt that way, I mean." She rejoined him at the table and tentatively reached for his hand. She was overjoyed when he grabbed it, but surprised by the strength of his grip. It was almost as if he were holding on to a lifeline. "Ted, I'm sorry I wasn't more sensitive to your feelings. I — I guess I figured you were so self-assured and everything that I could pour out all my anxieties and you'd be strong enough to handle them and yours all at once. We've got to start being honest with each other, Ted. If we're not, our relationship won't be worth anything." The teakettle began to whistle shrilly. Chris got up to turn it off and prepare the hot chocolate. Ted still hadn't said anything, so when she sat down again with the two steamy mugs she asked him a question that had been on her mind for weeks: "Do you resent that I got elected student body president?"

Ted put his hands around the cup and stared down into the steaming brown liquid. "Yeah," he answered. "Sometimes I do."

Chris had always heard that confession was good for the soul, but she was finding these moments among the most difficult of her life. She held her own cup tightly in both hands for support. "I never would have run if you hadn't turned down the nomination. If I were you I'd be questioning whether I made the right decision."

"That was the first time I ever realized I wasn't up to the challenge."

"Would it help if I quit?" Chris asked.

"I'd never ask you to do that," Ted answered quickly. "I know how much it means to you, and the truth is I never could have gotten as worked up about the job as you have. So it's for the best that you won." He took a deep breath and stared into her concerned eyes. "I don't know if Brenda told you, but I haven't been to baseball practice lately."

"I know. I went to the field yesterday."

Ted set his mug down hard on the table.

"It's getting hot in here," Chris said. "Do you want to go outside?"

"Sure." Ted followed her out the back door and toward Mrs. Austin's flower garden.

Chris reached down for a daisy and shook the few remaining raindrops off its white petals. "Look, Ted, just because you're questioning your ability to play ball doesn't mean the rest of your life's got to go down the tubes, too. By that I mean *me*, of course." She handed him the flower. "What I'm trying to say is, I love you, Ted. You, not your batting average. You're really a pretty terrific guy."

"Like how?"

"I'll never forget the note you gave me after my mother died." Again Chris felt her eyes moisten as she pictured the card. On the front was a color photograph of the ocean. Inside he'd written: *The beautiful things in this world live forever in our memories.* "We weren't even dating then, but you were still sensitive enough about my grief to share it with me."

"It was nothing. Anyone would have done that."

"No, Ted, you're wrong. A lot of people I thought were really good friends didn't do anything. It was almost as if they were afraid of my sadness or something." There was a flash of lightning, followed seconds later by a loud clap of thunder. Chris ignored it as she and Ted continued to walk around the yard. "I don't want to dwell on somber things, though. There's that playful part about you I like, too. Remember the time I told you I was in the mood for clams?"

Ted's eyes brightened at the memory. "And I drove you to the Eastern Shore to see if we could dig some up." He chuckled. "That was back when we first started dating."

"We haven't done anything silly like that in a long time," she said wistfully. "Let's go dig for clams."

Ted looked up at the dark gray sky. "No, the storm's not over yet. But I've got another idea."

"What's that?"

Ted pulled her close, tilting her head up to his. "There aren't many girls around who'd put up with a guy like me. I love you, Chris." Then right there in the middle of her backyard he kissed her. Chris fell into his arms willingly.

The next thunderclap was followed by a downpour so heavy that Chris couldn't even see the large apple tree just a few feet away from them.

Her black flats were getting soaked as they sank against the trunk of a large oak tree. The rain hit her forehead and dripped down the side of her face, running around her chin, where it fell drop by drop onto her chest. But none of that mattered as she basked in the warm cocoon of Ted's arms. She'd come so close to losing him that his embrace seemed even more special than usual.

Ted was in no hurry to leave either. "This is great," he shouted over the machine-gun patter of the rain hitting the nearby roofs. "I've never kissed a girl in the middle of a rainstorm before."

"I told you I was up for new experiences," she told him. Pointing to the ground she added, "Ever try mud wrestling?"

Ted held her even tighter to his chest and laughed. "Uh uh. I'm not trying any more new sports," he said. "Let's stick to what we're already good at."

"You mean this?" Chris pressed her lips tightly to his.

Chapter
20

". . . So Holly hands back my yearbook and I look down at her picture. She wrote, 'Thanks for the good times. I'll never forget them. Holly.' She tried to be original and that's what she comes up with." Brad snorted as he related the story to Peter, who had been doing his radio show and had missed the lunchtime autographing session.

The two boys had joined Chris, Brenda, and several of Ted's friends at Briarwood Park to watch him practice. The small entourage nearly filled the bleachers. With Chris's encouragement Brad had hand-lettered a sheet-sized sign that read WE LOVE YOU, TED, which was unfurled across the bottom row.

Brenda turned to Chris. "So where's Ted?"

"Number 33. In right field." Chris proudly pointed to Ted, who was playing catch with the center fielder. "Aren't the uniforms cute?"

Brenda smiled. "Maybe if Ted had modeled his uniform for you he would have saved himself a lot of grief."

"I wish it could have been that simple, Brenda. It was an awful way to get to where we are at this point, but I think we know each other a lot better now. And I have to admit I like him better, too. There's something about a guy who's man enough to admit he's vulnerable that makes him very appealing."

"You're pretty lucky, Chris," Brenda said.

The bleachers erupted in a giant roar. Chris's eyes darted to the field just in time to see Ted rolling around in the grass. When he got up he waved his glove triumphantly in the air, a small white baseball stuck in its webbing.

Chris let out a giant whoop. As far as she was concerned the smile on Ted's face was worth a million league championships or slots on triple-A teams. Terry Detroit, eat your heart out, she thought smugly.

As Ted's team came in from the field, he dropped his glove, then strode quickly toward home plate, picking up three bats and weighing them against each other as he walked. His friends shouted from the bleachers. Brenda tugged Chris's sleeve.

"Let's go watch from the fence."

They were walking toward the field as Ted took a mighty swing. The ball sailed high into the sky — then dropped into the waiting glove of the center fielder. Chris grabbed the wire fence tightly as Ted walked slowly back down the first baseline. She wanted to tell him it was all right, that a fly ball to the outfield could become a home run with practice.

She turned back to the bleachers where her friends were still applauding Ted's attempt. Justin Pratt never had this many Kennedy students show up to watch him pitch.

"Hey, what's with the down face?"

Chris felt a strong set of fingers grasp hers through the fence. "Ted!" she gasped. "I'm so sorry."

"About the out?" he pursed his lips. "Hey, come on, Chris, I'll get another chance. That's what the game's all about. Even the best hitters miss seven out of ten times."

"Get back out there and play ball," she said, squeezing his fingers. "And I do mean *play*. See you after practice."

"Can't wait," he said with a wink before trotting back to the players' bench.

Smiling, the two girls headed back to the bleachers. But after only a few steps they paused. In the distance someone was shouting, "Chris! Chris!"

Chris turned in the direction of the voice. It was her stepmother, running toward them from the parking lot. She was waving a white envelope in her hand.

"Chris!" she called again, getting closer and closer.

"Catherine, what are you doing here?" Chris started to feel nervous. All she could think was that something had happened to her father.

"I got home early today and found this in the mail. I didn't open it, but I thought you'd want to see it as soon as possible."

Immediately Chris spotted the congressional insignia on the return address. She was relieved Catherine's visit had nothing to do with her father, but a new set of jitters erupted as she tore the letter from her stepmother's hands.

She examined it closely, noting with dismay that it was too thin to hold more than one sheet of paper. Chris was afraid the news would be as stiff and formal as the college rejection letters some of her senior friends had received. *Dear Applicant, We're sorry to inform you. . . .*

Shaking the thought from her mind, she looked back at her stepmother. "Thanks for bringing it, Catherine," she said. Her fingers were fumbling clumsily as she tried to open it.

"I'm dying to know what's inside, too," Catherine said excitedly.

"If I can ever get it open. . . ." Chris muttered, nearly tearing the envelope in half. Her heart was pounding in overdrive. One way or the other, this was it, the answer she had been waiting for for so long.

Nervously she took the letter and began to read aloud, "Dear Ms. Austin. We're pleased to inform you that your application for an internship in the Rose Hill district office of Maryland Representative Michael Barnes has been accepted. Please report to the office at 9 A.M. sharp on — "

"Chris, you're in! You did it!" Brenda shouted happily.

"Congratulations, dear," Catherine said.

Chris looked at them incredulously. She couldn't believe it was true. "I got the job," she said softly. Then, having said it aloud, the true meaning of the words finally sank in. "I got the job!" she yelled at the top of her voice. She grabbed both of them, and the three of them did an impromptu dance right next to the fence.

The commotion brought her friends down from the bleachers. "You got it, didn't you, Chris?" Brad said. To her happy nod he replied, "I always knew you would."

"When do you start?" Peter asked.

"It's all in here," Brenda said, wrapping her arms around Brad. She took the letter from Chris's hand and gave it to the others to read.

Chris broke away from her family and walked toward the Ramblers' bench. Her happiness wouldn't be complete until she got the approval of the one person who really mattered.

She didn't have to go far. Several of the boys had stood up to see what all the noise was about. One of them had been Ted, who was now walking in her direction. Chris smiled at him and gave him a nod with her head. He responded with a thumbs-up sign and big smile of his own.

Chris couldn't have asked for anything more.

Running toward Ted at full speed, she threw herself into his arms. "Ted," she said quietly, "I have a feeling that this is the beginning of a terrific summer." From behind the fence, another round of applause erupted.

Coming Soon...
Couples #12
BAD LOVE

Brenda got off the bus and stepped into the warm sunshine. When she'd awakened, she had hoped that it would be a rainy day, but it turned out to be sunny and beautiful.

Not really caring what she looked like, she'd thrown on a pair of cut-off jeans, a huge T-shirt that reached to an inch above the frayed hem of the shorts, and leather strapped sandals. She wore Brad's earring in her left ear, and three very different earrings in her right ear.

Although it was early yet, Brenda could tell it was going to be a scorchingly hot day. When she arrived at Garfield House, she paused to look around. The familiar wallpapered hallway was filled with small groups of kids, most of whom she recognized.

On her way to a group session she was leading, Brenda passed a partially open door. In the opening, stood a tall, good looking boy with black, unruly hair. His eyes were dark and inscrutable, yet they seemed to be penetrating right into her very soul.

When their eyes met, Brenda shivered. His physical presence was powerful, almost overwhelming, and his piercing gaze made her feel strangely vulnerable. All at once Brenda felt uncomfortable, almost apprehensive, and she very nearly stumbled in her effort to take her eyes from him.

Who is he? she asked herself when she managed to make it back to her seat without falling.

The session lasted fifteen more minutes. But Brenda found it hard to concentrate. Whenever she looked at the door, she saw the boy hidden in the shadows, and her thoughts became confused. She wondered if anyone else had seen him, and then realized with a start that he was standing in a spot where only she could see him. Was he doing that on purpose? Who are you? she whispered to herself again and again.

But there was no answer, only a feeling of mounting fear and excitement.